NANCY DREW FILES

THE CASE: *Solve the 30-year-old mystery of Mayor John Harrington's death—did he jump or was he pushed?*

CONTACT: *Todd Harrington—the handsome young candidate who doesn't want the bizarre case of his father's death reopened.*

SUSPECTS: *Charles Ogden, the Harrington chauffeur. He disappeared shortly after John Harrington was found dead.*

Neil Gray, John Harrington's opponent in the race for governor. He had an appointment with the mayor the night he died.

Sam Abbott, now mayor of River Heights, was John Harrington's personal secretary.

COMPLICATIONS: *Brenda Carlton has challenged Nancy to a detecting duel that she's determined to win. Hannah Gruen seems to know more than she's willing to tell about Harrington's death. And someone's bent on removing Nancy from the investigation—permanently.*

Books in THE NANCY DREW FILES™ Series

Available from ARCHWAY paperbacks

THE NANCY DREW FILES™ CASE • 10

BURIED SECRETS

Carolyn Keene

AN ARCHWAY PAPERBACK
Published by POCKET BOOKS • NEW YORK

Distributed in Canada by PaperJacks Ltd., a Licensee
of the trademarks of Simon & Schuster, Inc.

AN ARCHWAY PAPERBACK *Original*

An Archway Paperback published by
POCKET BOOKS, a division of Simon & Schuster, Inc.
1230 Avenue of the Americas, New York, N.Y. 10020

In Canada distributed by PaperJacks Ltd.,
330 Steelcase Road, Markham, Ontario.

ISBN: 0-671-63077-6

First Archway Paperback printing April 1987

10 9 8 7 6 5 4 3 2 1

NANCY DREW, AN ARCHWAY PAPERBACK and colophon
are registered trademarks of Simon & Schuster, Inc.

THE NANCY DREW FILES is a trademark
of Simon & Schuster, Inc.

Printed in Canada

IL 7+

BURIED SECRETS

Chapter
One

SOMETHING WEIRD'S GOING ON here." Bess Marvin smiled and then glanced at her friend Nancy Drew. "Can you figure out what it is, famous detective?"

Eighteen-year-old Nancy Drew stuck her credit card back in her wallet, shook her reddish blond hair back out of her blue eyes, and looked around the River Heights shopping mall. Nancy *was* famous for her detective work, but at the moment she was more interested in new clothes than a new case.

"I've got it," Nancy said, slipping her wallet into her blue canvas bag. "I wasn't planning to come shopping today, but for once I've spent more money than you have, Bess. Even George has spent more money than you."

George Fayne, Bess's cousin, peered into her shopping bag and quickly looked up, surprised. "Nancy's right. I *have* bought more than you, Bess. Now, that is *really* weird."

"It may be weird, but it's not what I'm talking about." Bess glanced around the wide corridor of the mall. "This place is practically deserted," she complained. "Don't you think that's strange?"

"Well, what do you expect?" George asked. "It's spring. It's beautiful outside. Why should people want to spend time in here when they could be out jogging?"

Bess moaned. "You mean, if I want to see anybody interesting, I might actually have to take up jogging?"

"I've finally figured it out," Nancy said. "It's not that the mall is empty. It's just that it's empty of boys. Right, Bess?"

"Exactly," Bess agreed. "I haven't seen a single good-looking boy the entire time we've been here."

"I should have known," George said with a laugh. "You're not interested in shopping; you're interested in *who's* shopping."

"That's not fair. I'm interested in both," Bess

told her, heading for a shoe store. "Come on, help me pick out the right kind of shoes. If I have to go jogging to meet boys, I don't want to ruin my feet."

Bess was talking over her shoulder to her friends, so she didn't see the tall, dark-brown-haired boy coming out of the shoe store until she plowed into him, knocking him back against the plate-glass window. It was Ned Nickerson.

He straightened up and smiled down at Bess. "Hi, there. Fancy bumping into you, as they say." As he raised his head, his gaze wandered and his eyes met Nancy's.

When Nancy saw him, she stopped moving and returned his stare. Now what? she wondered nervously. Just a couple of months before, the two of them—who'd been going together "forever" as Bess put it—had split up. Nancy couldn't believe it had happened, and she also couldn't believe that they'd gotten involved with other people, but they had. Ned had even fallen in love with someone else.

But his infatuation was over now, Nancy knew, because just a few weeks before she and Ned had gotten back together—sort of, she reminded herself. We're not really back together; we've just decided to try again. It may not even work.

Trying not to look nervous, Nancy smiled and

quickly walked the rest of the way to the shoe store. "Hi, Ned," she said quietly.

"Hi." Ned had picked up Bess's shopping bag, and now he handed it to her, keeping his warm brown eyes on Nancy. "I'm surprised to see you here," he told her, making conversation. "It's such a great day, I thought you'd be doing something outside."

"It's all my fault," Bess said with a big smile. "I dragged her here—right, Nan?"

But Nancy and Ned weren't listening. Bess was wrong, Nancy thought, watching Ned. There is *one* good-looking guy at the mall today.

"So," Bess said to Nancy and Ned as she nudged George in the ribs, "why don't you two walk around while George helps me find some running shoes that won't give me blisters? We'll meet you at the car in an hour, if you're still around and want a ride home," she added with a knowing smile.

After George and Bess went into the store, Nancy and Ned remained standing still, staring at each other.

Come on, Nancy told herself. We'll never really get back together if we don't talk. "Listen," she said finally. "How about some pizza? I'm starving."

"I could go for some food," Ned agreed. "But let's eat it outside, okay? I've had it with being inside for today."

At the Pizza Spot Nancy and Ned each got a slice and then went out. A low brick wall divided the sidewalk from the huge parking lot, and they sat on it to eat, watching the shoppers come and go. They kept their conversation casual; Ned talked about how college was going. He was home for a short break. Nancy's father, attorney Carson Drew, had just left for a convention in Boston, so they talked about that, too.

It was not exactly a personal conversation, Nancy thought. But then, she decided, any conversation was better than none at all. At least they were together, and they were talking.

"Well," Ned said, tossing his pizza crust into a nearby trash can. "What do you—"

His words were drowned out by a blast from a loudspeaker. Looking up, Nancy saw a red, white, and blue van moving slowly through the parking lot. The voice from its loudspeaker urged everyone, "Come meet your next state representative, Todd Harrington!"

"I didn't think there were any Harringtons left in politics," Ned commented.

"I guess there'll always be a Harrington running

for something," Nancy said with a laugh. "River Heights wouldn't be the same without the Harrington family."

Harrington was a famous political name in Nancy's hometown. Maxwell Harrington, a wealthy and ambitious businessman, had started the political dynasty years before by getting himself elected to the town council, which he ran with an iron fist. But he had pinned his real political hopes on his son, John. And it was John who had made the Harrington name a household word.

While running for governor of the state, an election everyone was sure he'd win, John Harrington had died. His body was found at the bottom of the cliffs outside Harrington House, the family's enormous stone mansion overlooking the river. No one was ever sure how or why he'd died—the police had ruled it an accident or a possible suicide, but there was no note, and no reason why he'd kill himself. He was young, he was successful, and he was close to being elected governor of the state of Illinois.

Maxwell Harrington had died not long after his son, and after that, Harrington House was closed up. Because John Harrington's wife had died in childbirth, Todd was raised by his paternal grandmother in another town. Only a caretaker remained—the kind of caretaker who walked the grounds with guard dogs, chasing all trespassers from the property.

"Remember that time we took that walk in the moonlight at Harrington House?" Nancy asked.

Ned smiled. "Yeah. We saw the caretaker's flashlight moving through the trees and decided it was John Harrington's ghost. You ran halfway down the road before you remembered we had a car."

"Well, I seem to remember you were right on my heels," Nancy replied, playfully punching his arm.

Laughing, Ned grabbed her hand and pulled her toward him. As they came closer together, Nancy thought he was going to kiss her. Maybe that was what they needed, she thought. Maybe a good kiss would fix everything.

But just as Ned's face moved close enough to Nancy's to kiss, another blast from the loud-speaker made them both jump apart.

"Come and hear Todd Harrington speak!" the voice boomed. "Find out why we need a Harrington in the House!"

As Nancy and Ned watched, the slowly cruising van pulled to a stop. Two men jumped out and began setting up a small, portable platform while a small crowd gathered.

When Todd Harrington jumped out of the van

and stepped onto the platform, even more shoppers came out to watch him. Nancy could see why. Todd Harrington was extremely good-looking, young and tall, with thick dark hair and a charming smile. Nancy was sure he would have Bess's vote if she were there.

"It's great to be here today," Todd Harrington said. "As many of you know, I was born in River Heights. Even though I didn't grow up here, I still think of it as my hometown."

The crowd clapped politely, and Todd Harrington went on to give a short speech about why he wanted to be their representative. When he finished, he asked if anyone had questions.

"Mr. Harrington!" a voice called out. "I'd like to know if you have any plans to reopen the investigation of your father's mysterious death!"

Everyone turned to see who had asked the question. It was Brenda Carlton, a reporter for her father's newspaper, *Today's Times*, and a pain in the neck in several of Nancy's cases.

"Trust Brenda," Nancy muttered to Ned. "You can always count on her to ask an embarrassing question."

Todd Harrington *did* look embarrassed, but he gave Brenda Carlton a quick smile. "I'm afraid I don't see a connection between my campaign and my father's death thirty years ago," he said. "But since you asked, the answer is no. The River Heights police closed that case, and I don't see any reason to reopen it. I'm here as a candidate, not as a detective. Anyone interested in my father's death can read about it in back issues of the newspapers. Anyone interested in my campaign is welcome to ask me about it now."

No one else seemed to have any questions, though. And when Brenda realized she didn't have any competition, she went right on asking about the strange death of John Harrington.

Nancy felt a little sorry for Todd Harrington. She could tell he was fed up with Brenda, but he couldn't come right out and tell her to be quiet. After all, he was running for office and had to be polite, even to someone as pushy as Brenda Carlton.

"Brenda's going to keep at him forever," Nancy said to Ned. "Poor guy. By the time she's through, he'll wish he'd never come to River Heights."

"You're right," Ned agreed. "The only way he's going to get rid of our 'ace reporter' is to tell her he'll reopen his father's case. If he doesn't, she's going to keep buzzing him, like an annoying gnat. Anyway," Ned went on, "I've had enough of politics for today. How about you? Are you ready to go?"

"Sure." Nancy didn't have any plans, really,

and she wanted to find out what Ned had in mind. Maybe she could invite him back for something to drink, and they could sit out on the porch and talk. Or maybe they wouldn't go straight home at all. Maybe he'd drive her to the park next to the river, with those nice, secluded benches. They used to go there all the time. If they went there that day, who knew what might happen?

Slowly Nancy and Ned walked around the edge of the crowd until they were close to Todd Harrington's platform. The young candidate was still trying to convince Brenda that his father's "mysterious" death was not what he wanted to talk about, and he still wasn't having any luck.

Nancy glanced out at the audience, hoping Bess and George were there so she could let them know she was leaving. That was when she saw it—somewhere in the middle of the crowd, something shiny, something glinting in the sun.

Nancy blinked, rubbed her eyes, and squinted to get a better look. The sun flashed on the object again, and then whoever was holding it took a step forward.

And in that instant Nancy knew exactly what it was. It was the barrel of a gun, and it was pointing straight at Todd Harrington.

Chapter

Two

IN ONE MOTION Nancy dropped her canvas bag and leaped in the air, flying up toward Todd Harrington like a released spring. She hit the young candidate from the side. And just as she felt his knees buckle, she heard the gun go off.

Locked together, Nancy and Todd rolled off the edge of the platform and landed with a thud on the hard cement of the parking lot.

"What's going—" Todd started to say, but his voice was drowned out by the screams of the crowd.

"Sorry!" Nancy gasped. She scrambled to her feet and plunged into the crowd, heading for the

11

spot where she'd seen the gun. She knew that whoever had shot it wouldn't stick around, but maybe she'd get lucky and see someone running fast, trying to get away.

Unfortunately, *everyone* was running. It took Nancy forever just to get to the edge of the panicked, screaming crowd. When she finally did, she looked around, desperate to see which way the sniper might have escaped.

The parking lot was a sea of cars—any one of them would have made an excellent hiding place. Beyond the lot was a bus stop, from which two full buses were just pulling away. Next to the main entrance of the mall was a parking garage, four levels high. And finally there was the mall itself, with at least a hundred stores. Whoever had shot at Todd Harrington could be browsing through any one of them right then.

"Nancy!" Ned called, running up to her. "I just saw a policeman heading toward the garage, and a couple of Harrington's men ran into the mall. So let's check out the parking lot!"

Quickly, at first, Nancy and Ned walked up and down the long rows, peering into and underneath cars. But by the time they'd covered ten rows, they weren't moving very fast.

"I hate to say it," Nancy admitted in frustration, "but this looks hopeless."

Ned nodded. "If the police could seal off the parking lot, maybe we'd have a chance."

"Maybe," Nancy said. "But it's a little late for that. Whoever fired that shot is probably on the other side of town by now."

"I guess you're right," Ned said. "I wish I'd been paying more attention. But all I saw was you flying through the air." He grinned. "You move pretty fast for somebody without wings."

Nancy laughed. "Thanks. And thanks for helping me."

"Anytime," Ned told her, glancing at his watch. "Oh, no. I can't believe it! I completely lost track of the time. I've got to leave now. Do you want to come with me or wait and catch a ride with George?"

Nancy hesitated. If she didn't go with him, would he think she didn't care? "I really ought to go back to the Harrington van," she said. "The police will want a statement from me."

"I'm not thinking straight, I guess. Of course you'll be needed."

"I'll be home in a little while, I'm sure," Nancy told him. She was hoping he'd suggest that they get together later that day.

But Ned was frowning at his watch. "I can't believe I've got to get going just when everything's gotten so exciting. I have to pick my mother up, though. Her car's getting fixed and she's without wheels." He shrugged and started off at a slow jog. Then he stopped and ran back to Nancy. "Can I call you later?" he asked quietly.

"Sure," she said, smiling and looking down. All of a sudden she felt shy with him.

"You can tell me what happened here."

"Sure," Nancy said again, feeling strangely deflated.

By the time Nancy got back to the van, more policemen had arrived. The one who'd been there from the beginning waved Nancy over. She told them everything she'd seen, which wasn't much.

"Did anyone in the crowd see anything?" she asked.

One of the policemen shook his head. "We've talked to four different people and we've gotten four different stories. One guy swears it was the woman standing next to him, except that he wasn't anywhere near the spot where you saw the gun. Another guy says it was a little kid with a cap pistol."

"Was it?" Nancy asked.

"Hah. Some cap pistol," the policeman said. "It left a slug from a forty-five automatic in the side of that van." He sighed and shook his head again. "And the other two witnesses just saw people running."

"That's no help," Nancy remarked. "Every-body was running."

"You said it," he agreed. "Well, we'll keep on it, check the gun registrations. Maybe something'll turn up. Anyway, at least we don't have a dead body on our hands, thanks to you."

Nancy smiled and turned to Todd Harrington. Except for a tear in one knee of his pants, he looked fine. He didn't look happy, though, and Nancy didn't blame him. He'd just been shot at, and Brenda was still at his side, hounding him with more questions.

A man had just moved up to his other side. And as Nancy crossed in closer, she heard him say, "As assistant to the mayor of River Heights, I want to assure you, Mr. Harrington, that the mayor's office will do everything it can to help find the person who shot at you."

"Thanks, I appreciate it," Todd Harrington said, wrapping a handkerchief around his scraped hand.

"Mayor Abbott is outraged," the assistant went on, "that such a thing could happen in his peaceful town, and—"

"But *why* do you suppose it happened?" Brenda broke in. "Mr. Harrington, could it possibly have anything to do with the death of your father?"

"I'm sure it doesn't," Harrington said. He glanced around, obviously hoping that someone would rescue him from Brenda. When he saw Nancy, his eyes lit up. "Excuse me," he said, stepping away from the other two.

When Todd Harrington reached Nancy, he stopped and held out his hand. "I have to admit that when you first leaped on me, I was ready to have you arrested," he said with a smile. "But now all I want to do is thank you. You can knock me off a platform anytime."

Laughing, Nancy shook his hand. "Thanks," she said. "Let's hope I never have to do it again."

"Well, well," Brenda said, walking over to them. "If it isn't Nancy Drew, the heroine of the day."

"Nancy Drew?" Todd asked. "Is that your name?"

Nancy nodded.

"Good," he said. "Now all I need is your address. I'd like to send you a little something."

Nancy started to say he didn't need to, but Brenda broke in again. "Oh, you don't need an address, Mr. Harrington!" she said sarcastically. "Just write 'Nancy Drew, U.S.A.' I mean, everyone knows who Nancy Drew is."

"Everyone but me, I'm afraid," Todd admitted.

"Are you serious?" Brenda gave Nancy a sly

wink. "Why, Mr. Harrington, Nancy Drew is River Heights's famous girl detective. Isn't that right, Nancy?"

Nancy bit her lip to keep from saying something nasty, but Todd Harrington seemed impressed. "A detective?" he said.

"Amateur," Brenda pointed out quickly.

"No kidding!" Todd went on, ignoring Brenda. "Well, who knows? Maybe you'll help find whoever took a shot at me."

"I'll try," Nancy said with a laugh. "I can't resist a good mystery."

"I think you should let the police handle it," Brenda told her. "But if you want to solve a mystery, there's an even better one to work on—the strange death of John Harrington."

"Miss Carlton, I hate to be rude, but I wish you'd drop that subject," Todd Harrington said. "If there was anything strange about my father's death, I'm sure the police would have found it. It's past. It's over. Now, please leave it alone!" With a nod to Nancy, he walked off toward the van.

"Honestly, Brenda," Nancy said. "Why don't you just drop it? You've gotten a wonderful story today."

"Because it's so interesting," Brenda retorted. "I mean, look at the facts. The body of John Harrington was found at the bottom of the cliffs outside his family mansion. There was no suicide note. The man was just about to be elected governor of the state. He was also just about to become a father—Todd's father. You don't kill yourself when you're on top of the world."

"Maybe it was an accident," Nancy said. "Maybe he slipped and fell."

"You don't slip and fall out of a tower window," Brenda said.

"The tower window?" Nancy asked, picturing Harrington House in her mind. "That's where he fell from?"

"According to all the experts." Brenda looked infuriatingly smug. "What do you have to say about that, Detective Drew?"

"Well, I'm not sure," Nancy said honestly. "But don't you have a story to file, Brenda? You just witnessed an assassination attempt. What are you doing talking to me?"

Brenda looked startled. "Oh, you think you know everything, don't you?" she asked. But she was already cramming her notebook and tape recorder into her bag.

"See you soon," said Nancy, strolling away.

Once she was alone, she began to think about what Brenda had told her. If John Harrington had fallen from a tower window, the case was entirely different because you don't slip and fall from a window like that. You either jump—or you're pushed.

And now to find Bess and George. She was going to need that ride home after all.

Nancy went to bed thinking about John Harrington's death. But when she woke up, she was thinking about Ned. Why hadn't he called? Of course, all he'd said was "Can I call you later?" but Nancy couldn't help thinking he'd have called her that night. His break from college wasn't going to last forever.

But maybe, she worried, he didn't really want to work things out. Maybe he still thought her detective work would come between them. Nancy hoped not—because there was no way she was going to stop.

Nancy kicked back the covers in frustration and got out of bed. Still in her yellow thigh-length T-shirt, she did a few sit-ups, brushed her teeth, and went downstairs and into the kitchen.

Hannah Gruen, the housekeeper who'd been with the Drews since Nancy was three, was already there, unloading the dishwasher. When she saw Nancy, she smiled. "Good morning. You're up early."

"I know," Nancy said with a yawn. "I tried to sleep longer, but the sun was too bright." Still yawning, she poured herself a glass of orange juice and sat down at the kitchen table. But when she had unrolled the newspaper and seen the front page, she stopped yawning.

"Hometown Detective Saves Life of Harrington," ran the headline. Above that was a photo of Nancy and Todd Harrington shaking hands, and the story below it, with Brenda Carlton's byline, covered almost half the front page.

Nancy grinned. Brenda must have really hated having to mention me at all, she thought. She sipped some more juice and started to read the story, but the phone rang before she got very far. Hannah picked it up.

"It's Bess," Hannah said. "She's all excited about something—maybe she won the lottery."

"Nan!" Bess shrieked after Nancy had taken the phone. "Why didn't you tell us you'd saved his life? You didn't mention one word in the car about what you'd done. I suppose you had a reason to be quiet. But now you've got to tell me all the important stuff. Like, what's he like? Is he as gorgeous up close as he looks from far away?"

"He sure is," Nancy said, laughing. "Todd Harrington is definitely a hunk."

"And to think"—Bess sighed—"you got to shake hands with him. Maybe you can introduce me to him."

"I'll probably never see him again, Bess."

"Sure you will," Bess said. "You saved his life, so he owes you. And when he asks how he can repay you, just tell him you have this friend who's dying to meet him! Oh, by the way," she went on, "what are you going to do about Brenda? Are you going to accept?"

"Accept what? What are you talking about?"

"You mean you haven't read it? Nancy, just turn to the editorial page. Brenda's done it again!"

After Nancy had hung up, she flipped through the newspaper until she came to the editorial page. There was a column called "In This Reporter's Opinion." That day, "This Reporter" was Brenda Carlton.

"It seems to this reporter," Brenda had written, "that our famous local detective, Nancy Drew, should want to sink her teeth into a mystery that has remained unsolved in River Heights for the past thirty years—the death of John Harrington.

"But maybe our detective finds a mystery in her own hometown too boring. Maybe she's afraid she won't be able to solve what happened to John Harrington. Or maybe she's losing her touch.

"Is that true, Nancy Drew? This reporter hopes not, because she has decided to solve the mystery herself. And this reporter is challenging you to an 'investigative duel.' Do you accept, Nancy Drew? Or *have* you lost your touch?"

When Nancy finished reading, she didn't know whether to laugh or scream. She knew she wasn't losing her touch! But a "duel"? Nancy didn't want to get into that with Brenda.

Of course, the Harrington case *was* very interesting. It would be a challenge to try to find out exactly what had happened.

Nancy was still trying to decide what to do when the phone rang again. That time it was Ned.

"Hi," he said. "Sorry I didn't call you last night. I wanted to, but I got tied up with my family."

"That's okay," Nancy told him. At least he wanted to, she thought.

"I see you made the front page," Ned said. "And the editorial page, too."

"So you saw Brenda's challenge."

"She's got nerve, you have to give her that," Ned commented. "You *are* accepting, aren't you?"

Nancy wasn't sure whether Ned would like it, but she knew she couldn't resist. "I think I will," she said. "Brenda couldn't solve a mystery if she was handed all the clues. And besides," she added, "you know I love a good mystery."

"I remember," he said.

Nancy still wasn't sure whether he was happy about it, but what he said next made her happy.

"Just be careful," Ned told her softly. "I wouldn't want anything to happen to you. I'll call later when I know what my plans are. Okay?"

Still smiling, Nancy hung up. "Looks as though I'm on a new case, Hannah."

"Oh?" Hannah turned, holding two glasses in each hand. "Where will you be traveling to this time?"

"Nowhere," Nancy said, pointing to the newspaper. "The death of John Harrington is a home-grown, River Heights mystery."

Suddenly a glass slipped from Hannah's fingers, splintering on the hard tiled floor. But Hannah ignored the shards of glass at her feet. Her face white, her eyes wide, she stared at Nancy and shook her head.

"Stay away from that case!" she said in a shaky voice. "I beg you, Nancy, don't have anything to do with it!"

Chapter

Three

H<small>ANNAH</small>!" N<small>ANCY CRIED</small>. "What's wrong? Why should I stay away from the case?"

"I—I just mean that it's such an old case," Hannah stammered. "And it *was* solved, years ago."

"Maybe, maybe not," Nancy said. "But even if it turns out that he had just fallen, why don't you want me to get involved?"

Hannah reached for the dustpan and brush, and began to clean up the broken glass. "Oh, never mind me," she told Nancy. "I suppose I was just shocked to hear John Harrington mentioned again. After all, it was quite a big story back then."

"But, Hannah, you begged me not to get involved!" Nancy protested.

"Well, you know me. I always worry about you," Hannah said with a laugh. "Now let me get on with my chores, Nancy."

Nancy started to protest again, but then she changed her mind and headed for the bathroom to shower. Hannah obviously didn't want to talk anymore, and Nancy knew it was useless to try—right then.

"Well, well." Brenda Carlton stood up behind her desk at her father's newspaper office and smirked at Nancy. "Look who's here."

Two hours had passed, and Nancy decided to stop by the *Today's Times* office to let Brenda know she was going to accept the challenge.

"Don't tell me you let 'this reporter's opinion' bother you," Brenda continued.

"Of course not," Nancy said, trying to sound casual. "I'm a sucker for a challenge, you know that."

Brenda looked surprised. "You mean you're accepting?"

"Sure, why not?" Nancy sat on the edge of the desk and grinned. "What's the matter, Brenda? Are you scared you'll lose?"

"Don't be silly." Brenda tossed her hair back

and tried to smile. "After all, I already know ten times more about the story than you do."

"That won't last long," Nancy said. "Just give me a day to read the police files and the microfilms of the back issues of the newspapers, and we'll be even."

"Microfilms of back issues? Gosh, Nancy, I don't know about that," Brenda said. "I mean, we're not on the same team. Just because I work here doesn't mean I should make it easy for you by letting you look at all those old newspaper films."

"Oh, yes, it does," Nancy leaned closer to Brenda. "Because if you don't, I'll write a letter to the editor, and then I'll go to the public library to read them."

Brenda knew she didn't have any choice. "Well, all right." She pouted. "I guess it doesn't matter anyway. I'm already miles ahead of you."

"Good for you. But be careful not to stop and look over your shoulder," Nancy warned her. "That's how you *lose* races."

Without another word, Brenda grudgingly directed Nancy to the *Times*'s morgue, which was where all the microfilms of past issues were stored. With a little help, Nancy found all the films she needed and learned how to use the microfilm reader. She sat down at a long wooden table and started to read everything she could find about John Harrington.

An hour later she had learned some very interesting things. Todd had been born four months after his father's death; his mother had died giving birth to him. He'd been brought up by his paternal grandmother in another town. He'd lived in Harrington House for only his first month—the house had been closed up ever since then—but he'd inherited the house at the age of twenty-one.

No wonder he doesn't want all that stuff about his father dragged into the open again, Nancy thought. He will probably move back here someday, and he wouldn't want a big deal made out of his father's past.

She also learned that Sam Abbott, now the mayor of River Heights, had been John Harrington's personal secretary. He'd been with Harrington the night he was killed. But Abbott had never been suspected of anything, because the Harrington's chauffeur, Charles Ogden, said he'd spoken to John Harrington after Abbott had left the mansion.

Nancy made a note to speak to Mayor Abbott and to Charles Ogden, if he was still in River Heights. But the person she wanted to talk to most was Neil Gray, John Harrington's opponent in the race for governor. Neil Gray had had an appointment with John Harrington the night Harrington died. He claimed he'd never seen Harrington—that when he got to the mansion, Sam Abbott had met him and told him the meeting was postponed.

What made Nancy really want to talk to Neil Gray was something the newspaper said—that, according to Gray, the Harringtons had used every dirty trick in the book to ruin his name and campaign.

"They said I dropped out of college," he was quoted as saying. "But they didn't bother to add that I dropped out because I needed money to finish. And I did finish, fourth in my class.

"They said I was fired from the first law firm I worked for. What they didn't say was that the firm was dissolved. Nobody was fired—there just wasn't any firm to work for anymore.

"They accused me of accepting campaign money from criminals. That's true. One of the people who gave me money had two parking tickets."

Neil Gray had more stories to tell, and each one was worse than the last. He was an angry man, and if what he said was true, Nancy figured he had every right to be. But had he been angry enough to kill John Harrington?

Nancy glanced at her watch. It was twelve o'clock. With only half a glass of orange juice in her stomach, she was starving. But she decided to go to the police station before she ate because she wanted to read the files on the case to see if the police had been as suspicious of Neil Gray as she was.

Downtown River Heights was crowded with workers out for a quick meal or a stroll in the spring sunshine. Nancy was almost at the police station when the smell of hot dogs from an outdoor stand made her stop. Her stomach rumbled, and she couldn't ignore her hunger any longer. As she walked up to the hot dog stand, she saw she had an even better reason to stop—Ned was there.

Her heart pounding eagerly, Nancy sneaked up behind Ned. "I can't believe it," she said teasingly, "you still eat them with sauerkraut."

"Nancy!" Ned looked surprised and happy. "This is great. Tell you what—I'll buy your hot dog if you'll eat it with me in the park."

Nancy wanted to go, but she knew that if she did, she and Ned would hang out in the park for a while. "I'll make you another deal," she said. "You walk with me to the police station, and I'll buy my own hot dog."

"The police station?" Ned frowned. "You're on the case already?"

"Why not?" Nancy asked. "The faster I get on it, the faster I'll finish it." There, she thought, that ought to make him happy.

"I guess you're right," Ned agreed. "I just wish you had some free time. I'm going back to school in a few days."

Nancy's hot dog stopped halfway to her mouth. "Ned, I told you I was accepting Brenda's challenge and you didn't say anything! Now you're complaining. I don't get it."

"I'm not complaining," Ned protested. "I just want to spend some time with you, that's all."

"Well, why haven't you asked?"

"I was going to this morning, but you said you were accepting Brenda's challenge. And I didn't want to get in your way."

"Well, we're together now. Will you walk me to the police station?" Nancy smiled and took his hand. "Come on. We'll walk very slowly."

"Somehow I think I got the short end of this deal," Ned commented, but he did squeeze her hand. "Okay, you win. Let's go to the police station."

They did walk slowly, but the police offices were only a block and a half away, and it was hard to make the walk last more than five minutes. When they said goodbye, Nancy could tell Ned was disappointed. He's not the only one, she thought.

The mayor's office was right next door to the police station, and on the spur of the moment Nancy decided to go there first. As she entered the reception area, she could see the mayor in his office having what looked like a heated conversation with a tall, skinny man. The man's back was to her, and Nancy couldn't hear what he'd just said, but obviously it upset the mayor. Mayor Abbott's face turned red and he walked over and slammed the door of his office shut.

Politics, Nancy thought, and walked over to the secretary's desk. "Hi," she said, and gave her name. "I'd like to make an appointment to see Mayor Abbott."

The secretary peered over her glasses. "About what, dear?"

"About John Harrington's death," Nancy told her. "I'm investigating what happened that night, and I need to speak to everyone who was involved."

"Oh, dear, I don't know. Oh, well, the mayor will see anyone who asks. So I suppose I have to give you an appointment." The secretary sighed and flipped through her appointment book. The mayor had fifteen minutes of free time at the very end of the next day, and even though she still didn't look happy about it, the secretary made the appointment for Nancy.

Nancy thanked her and headed for the police station. Since she'd worked with a lot of the officers, she didn't have any trouble getting permission to look at their computerized files. But the files left her with more questions than answers.

Charles Ogden, the Harringtons' chauffeur, had left River Heights shortly after John Harrington's death, and there was no record of where he had gone. And even though Neil Gray had been a strong suspect, the police hadn't been able to pin anything on him. There was no address listed for him, either.

Nancy was disappointed—he had been her prime suspect. Then, just as she was about to shut off the computer, she noticed something. Two of Gray's campaign workers had been Gerald and Joyce Nickerson—Ned's parents.

Good, Nancy thought. I'll talk to Ned's parents, and I'll make sure to do it while Ned's home—at least we'll be together. She shut off the computer, and went to a pay phone in the hall. No one was home at the Nickersons'.

What now? So far, she had hundreds of questions and no answers. Then Nancy remembered Harrington House. Of course, she thought. The best place to start an investigation was at the scene of the crime.

* * *

A few minutes later Nancy's Mustang was smoothly climbing up the narrow winding road to the Harrington mansion. As Nancy drove, she kept catching glimpses of the massive house. Built of stone, it was three stories high and looked as long as a city block. At one end was a tower. Nancy knew it overlooked the cliffs leading down to the river. The circular tower room had two small windows facing the river; one of them was the window from which John Harrington had to have jumped or fallen. Catching another glimpse of the tower and one window, Nancy shook her head. It just wasn't possible to fall out of a window like that.

The road curved again, and the house was blocked from view by the many trees on the vast estate. Finally Nancy pulled up at the massive iron gates and got out.

The gates were locked, and the gatehouse beyond looked deserted. "Hello!" Nancy shouted. "Anybody in there?"

No answer. Nancy walked a little way back down the road, hoping to find an easier way to get onto the grounds than by climbing that enormous iron gate. But she couldn't see anything because a high masonry wall ran around three sides of the estate and blocked everything but the highest treetops.

Nancy moved off the road and into the woods, skirting the wall, until she saw the red-tiled roof of the tower, which loomed high above her. Nancy continued to move straight ahead a few more feet until she could hear the river far below. Cautiously walking to the edge of the cliffs, she stared down at the ragged ledge and sharp rocks where Harrington's body had been found.

Was it suicide? she wondered with a shudder. Or was it murder?

Before she'd finished the thought, Nancy felt a hand close tightly on her shoulder.

Chapter

Four

Nancy's reflexes took over. Grabbing the hand, she crouched slightly, then straightened, pulling whoever was behind her over her shoulder and flat onto the ground—only a few yards from the cliff edge. Gasping, she looked down and saw the dark brown eyes of Todd Harrington staring up at her.

"Mr. Harrington!" she cried. "I'm sorry, I—are you all right?"

Todd Harrington sat up slowly and rubbed the back of his neck. "I'm still in one piece," he said. "I think." Then he smiled. "This is the second time you've knocked me down! You're not only a detective, you're a judo expert."

"Not really an expert," Nancy said, holding out her hand to help him up. "I have a friend who is, though, and she taught me that move."

"Well, it's a good thing your friend wasn't here," Todd remarked. "I might not have survived her."

"I'm really sorry," Nancy said again. "I was just thinking so hard that I didn't hear you come up behind me."

"Next time I'll shout a warning," he said, and they both laughed. "Well," he went on, "I hope you don't mind if I ask what you're doing here. It's okay, of course, but I'm just curious."

"Did you see the paper this morning?" Nancy asked.

"Oh, no." Todd shook his head in disappointment. "Don't tell me you let that nosy reporter get to you."

"I'm afraid I did," Nancy admitted. "Besides, I think Brenda Carlton may actually be on to something. Lots of things about your father's death make me very curious."

"Such as?"

"Such as that window." Nancy pointed to it. "It's not a window you accidentally fall out of."

"What are you suggesting?" Todd asked with a frown. "Murder?"

"I'm not suggesting anything yet. I'd just like to

find out everything I can. That's why I came here today," Nancy explained. "I wanted to have a look around, but I couldn't get in."

"I'm surprised you didn't just climb over the gate."

"That was my next move," Nancy said with a grin.

"Well, I'd invite you in, but we're really up to our ears in work right now. I was just taking a breather when I saw you."

"We?" Nancy asked.

"My campaign staff," Todd explained. "We've taken over the house. We're using it as a base of operations, and tomorrow we start a town-by-town tour of this district. So we're running around like crazy, getting ready." He checked his watch. "My campaign manager's probably wondering where I am. Ever since that attempt on my life yesterday, I'm supposed to be kept under lock and key."

"Do the police have any clues or ideas yet?"

"No, they're hoping it was just a single crazy person acting on impulse and not a conspiracy. That way he won't try again."

"I guess you'd better get back, then," Nancy said, wishing he'd change his mind and ask her to come.

"Yes, but listen, Nancy," he said seriously. "I

have to tell you that I'd be a lot happier if you'd just drop this whole thing about my father."

"I can tell that," Nancy said. "But I don't understand why."

Todd looked toward the roof of the mansion and sighed. "I never knew my father, but I heard a lot about him growing up. And what I heard wasn't all good. He and my grandfather weren't exactly saints." He shook his head and sighed again. "They didn't like to lose, and they didn't like anyone who got in their way. I guess what I'm saying is that they played hardball, and they didn't always play by the rules."

Nancy nodded, remembering Neil Gray's accusations.

"So if all this stuff gets dragged through the papers," Todd went on, "it's going to make people start to wonder if I'm the same as they were. And it could ruin my campaign." He checked his watch again and then looked at Nancy. "You saved my life," he told her, "and I owe you one. But I wish you wouldn't go on with this investigation. I know I can't stop you, but I'm not going to help you, either."

Nancy nodded again, but didn't say anything. She was wondering about her own motives. She knew that part of her interest in the case was simply because *any* unsolved case was challenging.

And part of it—she hated to admit—was because she wanted to beat Brenda Carlton. But she also believed that finding the truth could be helpful in the long run. No matter what Todd thought about his father, he would probably want to see justice done. If he was an honest man, that is—and she felt that he was. And, finally, Nancy was certain Todd would prefer her investigation to Brenda's.

She watched as Todd Harrington walked up to the wall and pulled back two tall bushes that were growing next to it. Behind the bushes, part of the wall had crumbled, and Todd easily climbed over it and onto the grounds of Harrington House. The bushes sprang back into place, covering the break so that anyone who hadn't seen it would never know it was there.

But I know, Nancy thought with a smile. And I just found that other door.

Back in her Mustang, Nancy turned on the radio full blast and headed down the winding cliff road toward town. Her head was a jumble of unanswered questions.

Had John Harrington jumped out that window? If he had, there had to have been a reason. So far, no one had found one. If it was something like big money trouble, Mayor Abbott would probably have known, since he was Harrington's secretary. But Abbott had told the police he couldn't think of any reason why John Harrington would want to die.

That brought Nancy back to murder. If John Harrington had been as ruthless as Neil Gray seemed to think, then he must have made many enemies. Neil Gray was at the top of her suspect list right then, but she couldn't forget about Ogden the chauffeur either. If she could just find those two, she might get started.

Nancy was keeping her fingers crossed that Ned's parents would know about Gray, but what if they didn't? And what about the chauffeur?

Impatiently, Nancy flipped the dial on the radio. Hard rock was only making her head pound. She found a mellower station and tried to clear her head. But that didn't work, either.

Was Todd Harrington really afraid her investigation would hurt his campaign? Or did he know more than he was letting on?

And what about Hannah? Why had she been so scared about this investigation?

Nancy was thinking so hard that she didn't notice the car behind her until it bumped into the Mustang. "Hey!" she said out loud, honking her horn. "This is not exactly a good road for tailgating!" She tapped her brake, trying to get the car behind her to back off.

Instead, the car stayed on her tail, bumping the

Mustang again. This time Nancy knew it was deliberate. She glanced into the rearview mirror, but she couldn't tell who the driver was because of the sun. All she could tell was that the car was black.

Nancy tightened her grip on the steering wheel and pushed down on the gas pedal. The Mustang shot forward, its tires hugging the narrow road and squealing around the sharp turns. As soon as she hit a straight stretch, Nancy checked the mirror again. The black car was still behind her, inches from her car. And now there was another car behind it—a tomato red model that was staying very close to the black one.

What is this? Nancy wondered. Follow the leader? Another sharp turn was coming up, and she took it without braking. Her hands were sweating. Nancy loved to drive, but this ride was terrifying.

The road seemed to twist and turn endlessly, even though Nancy knew it was only a couple of miles long. She'd go around a turn, and the sun would almost blind her, so she'd have to slow down. And every time she came out of one of those turns, the black car would bump her from behind. It wasn't even a bump, really—it was more like a tap. But it was enough to make the Mustang rattle, and it was more than enough to make Nancy's knuckles grow white as she clung to the steering wheel.

Finally, up ahead, Nancy was able to see the last turn. Just hang on through that turn, she told herself, and after that when the road widens, you can pull over into the ditch if you have to.

In spite of the black car only a foot behind her, Nancy made the last turn safely. As she came out of it, she checked her mirror and saw that the tomato red car was still with them. Nancy didn't know if the two cars were together. And right at that moment, she didn't really care. All she wanted to do was lose both of them.

Up ahead, the road began to widen, and Nancy stepped on the gas. Just as she did, she saw a truck—a long, heavy gasoline truck—begin to lumber its way slowly across an intersection.

At the speed she was going, Nancy knew it would be only seconds before she rammed that truck broadside.

Chapter

Five

INSTINCTIVELY, NANCY WHIPPED her wheel to the right, jamming on the brakes and sending the Mustang into a wild spin. She knew her car might turn over, but even that would be better than plowing into a gasoline truck.

The Mustang rocked and squealed and spun around twice, but it stayed on the ground. And it missed the truck, which was still inching its way across the road.

Gasping, Nancy looked out, certain that her pursuer would never be able to swerve in time. She expected to hear the horrible sounds of a crash any second. Instead, the black sedan flew by

Nancy's car, cut to the left, and zipped around the back end of the truck, still going at top speed. Soon it was out of sight on the other side of the intersection.

Nancy took a shaky breath and was just about to let go of her steering wheel when the sound of squealing brakes made her cringe again. The red car, she thought. I forgot all about it!

In a flash the red car roared past, and as it did, Nancy caught a glimpse of the driver's panicked face. It was Brenda Carlton, her black hair blowing wildly and her red-painted mouth open in a scream.

Before Nancy had time to wonder why Brenda had been following her, the red car came to a screeching halt, just inches from the back of the gasoline truck. The truck, its lethal load untouched, continued to slowly move on.

Nancy started the Mustang and pulled to the side of the road. Then she got out and waited, her eyes blazing, while Brenda moved out of the intersection.

Brenda's face was white when she walked over to Nancy, and her usual sneer was missing. But Nancy couldn't feel much sympathy. She was furious.

"What kind of game are you playing, Brenda?" she demanded. "You could have gotten us all killed! And don't pretend you don't know what I'm talking about. I know you were following me."

Brenda swallowed and brushed her hair out of her eyes. "Well, it's true, *I* was following you," she admitted. "But I didn't know about the other car."

"What do you mean, you didn't know?" Nancy asked. "You were right behind it."

"I mean, I don't know who it was," Brenda explained.

"Why don't you just tell me what you were up to?" Nancy said.

"Okay." Brenda took a deep breath. "Just by accident I saw you come out of the police station and get in your car, and I followed you. On the way up to the Harrington mansion, I passed the black car, but I didn't think anything about it. When I got to Harrington House, your car was there, but you weren't, so I decided to leave."

"Why?"

"Well, there's no place to hide up there," Brenda said. "If I'd parked and waited for you, you would have seen me. Anyway," she went on, "I went a little down the road and found a place just wide enough to turn around in. So I parked there and waited for you."

The black car must have done that, too, Nancy

thought. The cliff road had more than one of those little turnarounds. "Well?" she said. "Then what?"

"Then I saw your car coming back down. I waited a few seconds and was just about ready to pull out when the black car came zooming past." Brenda shrugged. "I figured it was following *you,* so I followed *it.*"

"It wasn't just following me!" Nancy said. "Whoever was driving it wanted to run me off the road."

"Maybe not," Brenda said. "After all, I saw what was going on. If that car had wanted to run you off the road, it could have. But it didn't. Maybe the driver was just trying to scare you so you'll stay away from the Harrington case." She reached into her pocketbook for a brush and began fixing her hair. "You see?" she said with a pleased smile. "I was right—there *is* a mystery about this case. And somebody wants to cover it up."

"Okay, so let's play detective," Nancy suggested with a grin. "What was the make of the car?"

"Um—" Brenda frowned. "I'm not too good with cars. But it was a pretty new model, I think."

"Well, then, how about the license number?" Nancy asked. "Did you get that?"

Brenda zipped up her pocketbook, looking almost embarrassed. "Well, not all of it," she admitted. "I mean, we were all going so fast, and I was having enough trouble staying on the road. But I'm almost positive it started with a three."

"Great." Nancy shook her head in disgust. "That really narrows it down, Brenda."

"All right, you don't have to rub it in." Brenda frowned, then tossed her hair triumphantly. "I *can* tell you this, though," she said. "The driver was a man."

"Are you sure?"

"Please, Nancy, I do know a man from a woman!" Brenda said indignantly.

"Okay." Nancy nodded. "What else did you notice about him?"

Brenda sighed impatiently. "I didn't have all day to look, you know. But I did notice that he was tall. His head nearly reached the ceiling of the car."

A tall man, Nancy thought. Great! I only know thousands of them.

"Well," Brenda said, "if you're all through cross-examining me, I think I'll go."

"Just one more thing," Nancy told her. "You haven't explained *why* you were following me."

"Isn't that obvious? I wanted to see if you'd gotten any leads." Brenda smiled nastily. "After

47

all, in a contest it's always important to know what your opponent's up to."

"The older Harringtons would have liked you a lot," Nancy commented.

"What's that supposed to mean?"

"It means you don't play fair," Nancy said. "And you'd better not follow me again," she warned, "or I'll let everybody know what you've been doing."

"Honestly, Nancy." Brenda waved her hand at their two dust-covered cars. "Do you really think I want to get into another high-speed chase? I'd have to be crazy. Don't worry, from now on if anyone's following you, it won't be me."

With a final toss of her head, Brenda strutted over to her car, got in, and drove off without a backward glance at Nancy.

Nancy almost laughed. Some detective, she thought. She's following a car that's trying to run me off the road and she doesn't even bother to check the license number.

But Brenda was right about one thing. Someone was trying to stop Nancy's investigation. All Nancy had to do was figure out who.

Suddenly a loud whistle made Nancy look up. A car, filled with boys, was going by, and all of them waved wildly at her, whistling and asking if she needed a lift.

Smiling, Nancy shook her head and then got into the Mustang. If she was going to do any thinking, the side of the road was not the best place to do it. A hot shower, she thought. That was always a good place for a brainstorm.

On the way back, Nancy drove by the Nickersons' house, hoping to ask about Neil Gray. But no one was there, so she went home and jumped into the shower.

Who knew that she was investigating the Harrington death? That was obviously the place to start. Nancy stood under the warm spray and thought about it. Brenda, for one. And whomever Brenda had told—which was probably at least a hundred people.

Ned knew, and so did Hannah. But had Hannah told anyone? Nancy would have to ask her.

Then there was Todd Harrington and whomever he'd told. Todd didn't want her investigating his father's death, he'd admitted that. He said he couldn't stop her, but that didn't mean he wouldn't try. And of course, there was everybody she'd spoken to at the police station, plus the mayor's secretary. And probably Mayor Abbott, if he'd checked his appointment book for the next day.

And what about Neil Gray and Charles Ogden? If they were still in River Heights, they might know what she was doing. But if they were still in town, why didn't anyone know it?

Nancy turned off the faucets. The shower had felt great, but it hadn't produced any brainstorms. Not that time.

Nancy was just stepping out of the bathroom when she heard the phone ring. With a fluffy towel wrapped around herself, she dashed out of the bathroom and into her bedroom. She picked up the bedside extension on the fourth ring.

A male voice said, "Hi, sweetheart. How's business?"

"Dad!" Nancy cried. "I'm really glad you called. How are you? How's Boston?"

"I'm fine, and it's rainy," Carson Drew said with a laugh. "How are *you?*"

"Great," Nancy told him. "I'm on a case."

"Oh? Then why aren't you out solving it?" he asked.

Nancy laughed but decided not to tell him about her wild ride down the cliff road. "I *was* out," she said, "but I don't think I can get much more done today. I'm investigating John Harrington's death," she went on. "Do you remember it?"

"I guess so," Mr. Drew said. "Oh, yes, now I do—well, kind of. It was in the papers for weeks. And I remember it wasn't exactly settled or people weren't satisfied with the solution. Something like that."

"Were you satisfied?"

"Well, I don't really remember. Refresh my memory about the case." Nancy told her father what she had learned, and he said he couldn't believe John Harrington had jumped to his death. Mr. Drew became thoughtful. "To tell you the truth, he sounds so arrogant that I can't believe he'd kill himself."

"And he couldn't have fallen, either," Nancy said. "Not out that window."

"I see you *have* been on the case," her father commented. "Do you think he was murdered?"

"I don't know what I think yet," Nancy said. "Listen, Dad, do you remember Neil Gray?"

Carson Drew sighed. "Not really. How was he connected?" Nancy explained and suddenly her father did remember him. "I didn't think much of him."

"Oh? Why not?"

"I seem to remember he always had a chip on his shoulder. Remember, I was kind of young at the time—I don't have total recall about him or any of this."

A chip on his shoulder, Nancy thought. Neil Gray is definitely worth finding. "One more question, Dad."

"Shoot."

"John Harrington had a chauffeur. A man named Charles Ogden." Nancy crossed her fingers. "Did you know of him? Or anything about him?"

Her father laughed. "You're talking to the wrong person, Nancy."

"What do you mean?"

"Why don't you ask Hannah?" Carson Drew suggested. "After all, she and Charles Ogden were going together then."

Chapter

Six

H ANNAH!" NANCY ALMOST dropped the phone. "Hannah was going with John Harrington's chauffeur?"

"That's right," her father said. "This was before she married Mr. Gruen, and before she came to work for us, of course. But they had been going together. In fact," he added, "I'm pretty sure they had planned to get married."

Nancy's mind was whirling. If Hannah had known Charles Ogden then, she might know where he was now. And he just might be the reason Hannah wanted Nancy to stay off the case. "I wonder why they didn't get married."

"I don't know," Mr. Drew said. "In all the years I've known Hannah, she only spoke to me about him the one time. It was obvious she didn't want me to pry, so I never asked. In fact, you probably shouldn't mention to her that we had this talk. She might feel betrayed."

But *I* have to ask, Nancy thought. I just hope she'll talk to me.

"Well, it sounds as if you've got your hands full there," Carson Drew went on. "Be careful and let me know what happens. And remember about Hannah."

"I will, Dad," Nancy promised. "I'm glad you called."

After she hung up, Nancy sat on her bed, thinking about Hannah. She didn't know what surprised her more—the fact that Hannah had once had a boyfriend—other than Mr. Gruen, of course—or the fact that Hannah's boyfriend had been Charles Ogden.

Don't be stupid, Nancy, she told herself. Why shouldn't Hannah have had a boyfriend? She was young once, and she must have been good-looking. Guys probably had fallen all over themselves whenever they had seen her.

But Hannah had fallen for Charles Ogden. The same Charles Ogden who drove for the

Harringtons and then left town right after the police investigation. Had Hannah known why he left? Was that why she had been so afraid when Nancy mentioned the case?

Nancy got up and stepped into a pair of jeans. She'd just pulled a big, purple sweatshirt over her head when she heard the kitchen door slam. Hannah, she thought, home from the supermarket.

Barefoot, Nancy padded down the stairs and into the Drews' bright kitchen. Three grocery bags were on the table, and Hannah was standing at the refrigerator, putting away milk and eggs and vegetables.

"Hi," Nancy said. "Want some help?"

Hannah smiled. "Try the middle bag," she suggested. "It's got the pretzels in it."

Nancy found the bag and dug in. One hand full of pretzels, she used her other one to stack cans of tuna and tomato sauce in the pantry.

When the two of them were finished putting the groceries away, Nancy grabbed another handful of pretzels and sat down at the table. "Hannah," she said seriously, "there's something I want to talk to you about."

"Oh?" Hannah's eyes showed concern. "Nothing's wrong, I hope."

"No, not really." Nancy played nervously with a pretzel. "Look, I promise I wasn't trying to, but I accidentally found out about you and Charles Ogden."

Hannah closed her eyes for a moment. When she opened them again, Nancy couldn't tell what she was thinking.

"Hannah, I'm sorry to have to ask," Nancy said, "but whatever you know about him could be important. Please, won't you tell me what you can?"

Hannah took a long time thinking about it, but finally she nodded and sat down at the table. "I should have known that if you were on the case, you'd find out," she said with a small smile. "All right, what do you want to know?"

"Whatever you can tell me."

Hannah thought for a minute. "I'd been dating Charlie for almost a year," she said quietly, "when he started talking about our getting married. But, we couldn't get married right away—we needed to save money for a home first."

Nancy smiled. "Did you want to marry him?"

"I thought I did, at the time." Hannah got up and poured two glasses of iced tea from the refrigerator. She took a sip of hers and then went on. "Charlie had a plan. He'd been working for the Harringtons for a while, and he said they seemed pleased with him. So he was going to ask them for a raise."

"And what happened?" Nancy asked.

"John Harrington refused," Hannah told her. "Charlie came to me that night—the night Mr. Harrington died—and told me what had happened. He was upset, naturally. But by the time he had to get back to Harrington House, he was calm. We'd talked it all out and decided it wouldn't hurt us to wait awhile longer to get married."

"Charles never told you anything about what he saw when he went back to Harrington House?"

"Nothing," Hannah said quickly.

Had Charles really calmed down about not getting the raise? Nancy wondered. Or could he have been angry enough to kill Harrington? The only problem with that was that Ogden had driven Mayor Abbott home that night, and the mayor had confirmed it.

"Hannah," she said, "do you mind if I ask you why you and Charles never did get married?"

Hannah stood up, picked up her empty glass, and put it in the dishwasher. "Things just didn't work out between us," she said over her shoulder. "That's all. You know, sometimes you think a person is the only one for you, and then after a while you discover he's not. If I'd married Charlie,

57

I'd never have met Mr. Gruen—and I had a wonderful marriage with him. Now," she said briskly, "I'm going to go out in the yard and see if the ground's ready for the peas and carrots."

"Okay, Hannah. Thanks for talking to me."

"Of course."

"By the way," Nancy said, watching Hannah pull on her gardening gloves, "was Charles Ogden good-looking?"

"Oh, yes." Hannah smiled, as if she could see him. "He had bright black eyes and wavy dark hair and a dimple in his chin. All the girls were crazy about him, but he used to laugh when anyone told him he was handsome."

"He did?" Nancy asked. "Why?"

"Because he was short," Hannah said, heading for the back door. "He couldn't have been more than an inch taller than I am."

"So he was short," Ned said, taking a slice of pizza with everything on it. "All that means is he wasn't driving that black car today. He still could have killed John Harrington."

"I know," Nancy agreed. She picked a mushroom off her pizza and popped it into her mouth. "I guess it was too much to hope for."

Nancy and Ned were in Dino's, River Heights's

busiest pizza place. After talking to Hannah, Nancy had driven over to the Nickersons' and talked to Ned's parents about Neil Gray. They had worked for Gray's campaign because they were against John Harrington, but they'd thought Gray was a very unpleasant man. "Always looking over his shoulder," Mr. Nickerson said. "Always thinking everybody was out to get him."

Nancy had thanked them. Then, because she was hungry, and because she had wanted to be with him, she invited Ned to Dino's so she could tell him everything she'd learned about the case. What she wound up telling him was everything she *hadn't* learned.

"Your mother doesn't know where Neil Gray is," she said. "Your father doesn't know where Neil Gray is, and Hannah doesn't know where Charles Ogden is."

"Well, cheer up," Ned told her. "At least my parents said that Neil Gray was tall."

"Tallish," Nancy reminded him. "Your mother said tallish. He doesn't sound like somebody whose head would graze the roof of a car."

"You only have Brenda's word for that," Ned pointed out. "And she's hardly the most reliable witness."

"I suppose." Nancy frowned at her pizza slice,

which was now picked clean of everything but the cheese. Shaking her head, she took a new slice and bit into it. "Let's forget the case for now," she said. "Let's enjoy Dino's."

Ned leaned back and looked around. Dino's was packed and noisy as usual, with young people laughing and calling to one another, and the jukebox playing full blast.

"Uh-oh," Ned said suddenly. "I'm not sure we're going to be able to enjoy Dino's after all. Look who's here."

Nancy looked in the direction he was pointing and saw Brenda Carlton, her black hair gleaming against a red silk blouse, heading for their table.

"Well, Nancy," Brenda said, "taking time off from the case? I'm surprised at you."

Nancy took a sip of soda and tried to ignore her, but Brenda obviously had something on her mind. "I wouldn't waste too much time if I were you," she went on. "You just might find I've solved the case while you were taking a pizza break."

"What's that supposed to mean?" Nancy asked.

"It means I've got a lead," Brenda told her. "An important lead. It's too bad we're rivals, isn't it? Otherwise I might let you in on it." With a gloating smile, Brenda left the table.

"I just lost my appetite," Nancy said as she watched Brenda walk away.

"Don't believe a word she says," Ned advised. "She's just trying to get to you."

"I know," Nancy agreed. Still, she couldn't help being curious. Had Brenda really discovered something important about the case? "I really am finished eating, though," she told Ned. "As soon as you're done, we'll go."

Nancy was quiet as she drove Ned home. Finally he said, "Hey, Nancy, can't you forget about the case just for a little while?"

Nancy looked over at him, wishing he didn't know her so well. You've done it again, she told herself. Gotten so involved in a case that you practically forgot he was there. "Sorry," she said. "I *was* thinking about the case, but I was thinking about Hannah, too. Something she said was kind of sad."

"What was it?"

"When I asked her why she and Charles Ogden never married. She said that things like that happen. You think someone is perfect for you, and then after a while, you find out he's not."

Pulling up in front of the Nickersons' house, Nancy glanced at Ned again. What Hannah had said made her wonder if that was what Ned was feeling about her. Something was still missing in their relationship. They just weren't as close as they had been. Nancy couldn't help wondering if

Ned had decided that she wasn't the one for him anymore.

"Well, I guess things like that do happen," Ned said. "And it *is* sad, but it's better to find out sooner rather than later, right?"

Nancy nodded, feeling miserable. "Right."

"Anyway, thanks for the pizza, Nancy. And remember, don't let Brenda Carlton get to you." Ned started to open his door, then leaned across the seat and gave Nancy a kiss on the cheek. "See you," he said. Then he got out, slammed the door behind him, and trotted up the sidewalk to his house.

Well, he did kiss you, Nancy thought as she drove home. Somehow, though, a brotherly kiss didn't exactly make her want to jump for joy. By the time Nancy pulled the Mustang into her garage, she was furious with herself.

You should have grabbed him and kissed *him*, she thought, climbing out of the car. Who says you have to wait for him to make the first move?

Disgusted with herself, Nancy pushed the button to lower the garage door. It came down with a screech and a thump. As it settled into place, the garage went completely dark.

Groping, Nancy made her way along the wall, searching for the door that led into the house.

Then she heard it—by the workbench on the other side of the garage—a shuffling sound of someone moving, and then the sound of someone breathing.

Nancy froze. She wasn't alone in the pitch-black garage. Someone was with her.

Chapter

Seven

FOR A MOMENT the garage was completely still, except for the sounds of two people breathing. Nancy knew she was only a few feet away from the door into the house, but she wasn't sure she should run for it. Whoever was with her might have a gun, and once she opened the door, the light from inside would make her a perfect target.

Trying to keep her voice from shaking, Nancy called out, "Who's there? What do you want?"

"I came to warn you, Miss Drew." The whisper was deep and harsh, and it made Nancy shiver.

"Warn me about what?" she asked.

"The Harrington case. It could be dangerous."

"You mean I might get hurt, and you wanted to warn me about it?" Nancy said. "I guess I should be grateful, but somehow, trapping me in my own garage doesn't seem like a friendly warning."

"This isn't a joke, Miss Drew." The voice was still a whisper, but Nancy could hear the anger in it. "Stop your investigation of John Harrington's death."

"Why should I?"

"It belongs to the past. It's over and done with."

Hah! Nancy thought. If it's over and done with, then why are you so upset about it?

"Enough lives have been ruined," the voice went on. "Stop your investigation now."

"And if I don't?" Nancy asked.

There was a soft chuckle. "You said it earlier—you might get hurt. *Your* life might be ruined, too."

By then Nancy's eyes had gotten used to the dark, but even though she could make out the shape of the workbench, she still couldn't tell exactly where the man was.

"Now," the voice said, "I want you to do just as I say. If you do, you won't get hurt—not tonight, anyway."

Thanks a lot, Nancy thought.

"Get in your car," the voice directed, "and lie facedown on the front seat. When you hear the garage door open, don't look up. Remember, I'll be watching you. If you look up, you'll wish you hadn't."

Slowly Nancy felt her way across the floor to her car. Opening the door, she crawled in and stretched uncomfortably across the seats. The gearshift was jabbing her in the ribs. I'll do this, she thought, but there's no way I'm not going to look up when that door opens.

In another few seconds, Nancy heard clanging and whirring as the garage door lifted. She forced herself to count to three. Then she lifted her head just in time to see a crouched, shadowy figure slip under the door.

Quickly Nancy slid out of her car and ran out to the driveway. The neighborhood was quiet and well lit by streetlights and a few porch lights. But as far as Nancy could tell, she was the only person around.

A rustling sound made her jump. She whirled around, expecting to see someone creeping along the side of the house. Instead, she saw only the shrubbery blowing in the light wind.

You should have moved faster, she told herself. She walked down the driveway to the street, hoping to see someone fleeing the neighborhood, but she knew it was useless. Her nighttime visitor was long gone.

Carefully Nancy locked the garage door and went into the house. As she walked into her room, a thought suddenly hit her. If somebody had threatened *her,* had he threatened Brenda, too?

You should call her, Nancy told herself. If Brenda had gotten cornered in a dark garage by a stranger with a deep-throated whisper, she'd probably collapse and be out of commission for a week.

Having Brenda off her back for a week wasn't such a bad idea, actually! Still, Nancy went to the phone, found the number, and dialed.

"I don't know what you're talking about," Brenda said after Nancy had explained why she'd called. "Nobody's told me to stay away from the Harrington case."

"Well, just keep your eyes open," Nancy suggested. "This is my second warning, remember? The first one was on the cliff road today."

"But I don't get it." Brenda sounded indignant. "Why haven't I gotten a warning, too?"

Probably because you're not much of a detective, Nancy thought. Out loud, she said, "I don't know, Brenda. I just thought I ought to let you know what's happened."

"Well, I suppose I should thank you," Brenda

said, trying to sound grateful. "But no one's going to stop me from solving this case."

No one's going to stop me, either, Nancy thought as she fell into bed. I don't care if it's Neil Gray or Charles Ogden or Todd Harrington or even the mayor of River Heights. No one is going to keep me from figuring this one out.

The next morning Nancy was sitting in the kitchen, eating an English muffin and trying to decide what to do. So far, she'd had no luck finding Neil Gray or Charles Ogden, but at least she knew where Mayor Abbott was. The problem was, her appointment with him wasn't until the afternoon, and she hated wasting a whole morning without following a single lead.

The doorbell rang, and when Nancy answered it, she was surprised to see a mailman standing there.

"Express letter for Miss Nancy Drew," he said.

"That's me," Nancy told him. She took the letter and closed the door, wondering if it, too, would be another warning.

The letter read: "Thanks again for your flying leap. If I ever get elected, want to be my bodyguard? Todd Harrington."

Nancy laughed. Todd's a real charmer, she thought. She just hoped he was sincere and that he wasn't the one who was trying to stop her from investigating his father's death.

Then Nancy remembered—Todd had left that day for a town-by-town campaign tour of his district. She wanted to have a good look around that tower office, and with Todd gone, she could get into Harrington House without his even knowing about it.

Half an hour later, dressed in a khaki safari jumpsuit with a canvas belt, Nancy was back in the Mustang, heading toward Harrington House. Remembering the day before, she kept a close eye on every black car she saw, but as far as she could tell, none of them followed her. She kept a lookout for Brenda's red tomato, too. She wouldn't put anything past Brenda Carlton.

But it wasn't Brenda Nancy saw as she drove near to the cliff road. It was Bess and George, in bright-colored sweat suits, jogging together along the street where the gasoline truck had just missed getting blown up. Actually, Nancy noticed, it was George who was doing the jogging. What Bess was doing could only be called a shuffle.

Pulling up to the side of the road, Nancy stuck her head out the window and called, "Hey! Need a ride?"

George, her dark hair bouncing, waved and kept trotting in place, but Bess stopped completely. Her lavender sweat suit was drenched, her blond hair was tangled, and her cheeks were as red as Brenda Carlton's car.

"Nan," Bess said breathlessly, "you'll never know how glad I am you came by. We've been jogging for hours, and I haven't run into a single good-looking guy yet. I've been breathing so much dust I'm choking, and I'm totally wiped out."

"We've only been jogging for fifteen minutes," George told her. "And you said you wanted to keep going."

"That was before I saw Nancy's car," Bess said. "Now that I've seen it, I'm ready to collapse."

"Well, okay," George agreed as they walked over to climb in. "I guess you shouldn't go too long the first day out, anyway."

"First day and *last* day," Bess moaned, collapsing into the seat.

Laughing, Nancy told her friends where she was going. Immediately they wanted to come along. As she drove, Nancy filled them in on everything that had happened so far.

"He was waiting for you in the garage?" Bess said, her eyes wide. "I would have panicked."

"I almost did," Nancy admitted. "But I had the feeling he wasn't out to hurt me. Whoever it was just wanted to scare me off."

"But what happens when he finds out you're *not* scared off?" George asked.

"I don't know," Nancy said. "I just have to hope I find him first, I guess."

Nancy didn't bother going all the way to the iron gates. She pulled the Mustang into one of the small turnaround spaces in the road.

"Don't tell me we have to hike the rest of the way up," Bess said.

Nancy laughed. "Actually, yes, but it's only a short distance. You might have to climb a bit, though," she told her. "Are your feet up to it?"

"Actually, I'm feeling okay now. And," Bess added, "with a little food, I'll be completely recovered."

"Food?" George asked. "Who's got food?"

"I do." Bess reached under her sweatshirt and pulled out a small leather bag that she'd strapped around her waist. "I have two chicken sandwiches in here," she said. "I always come prepared."

The three friends got out of the car and followed the wall to the spot where Nancy had seen Todd Harrington's "second door." Pulling back the shrubbery, Nancy waved at the crumbling wall.

"This isn't exactly the way to go to somebody's house," George said jokingly.

"I know," Nancy agreed. "But I don't want anyone to see me going in. Besides," she added, "it's easier than climbing those front gates."

"That's fine with me," Bess said, putting one foot on a rock. "Come on, I'm dying to see this place."

The wall was easy to climb. In just a couple of minutes, the three girls had dropped softly onto the velvety grass of the Harrington House grounds.

But before any of them could take a step, two dogs came bounding out of a stand of trees, heading straight for them. The dogs were Doberman pinschers, black and lean and fast, and as they got closer, the girls could see that their fangs were bared.

They were ready to attack.

Chapter

Eight

INSTANTLY THE THREE girls started scrambling back up the wall.

"I just decided I love jogging!" Bess gasped. "In fact, I think I'll run all the way home!"

"I didn't know they had attack dogs!" Nancy cried.

"Well, those dogs aren't going to give up," Bess said. "They look as though they're ready to climb right after us. George, why don't you try one of your judo moves on them?"

"I hate to tell you, but I've never used judo on a dog," George said. "And I don't think I want to try now."

The girls were almost over the wall when they noticed that the dogs weren't barking anymore. Nancy looked over her shoulder, and what she saw made her laugh. "Bess," she said, "your lunch may have saved our lives."

In the rush to get over the wall, Bess's leather bag had fallen and the sandwiches had spilled to the ground. The two dogs were now feasting on chicken, totally ignoring the terrified girls.

"I'm glad it's chicken and not us," Bess commented. "Come on, let's get out of here."

"Wait a second," George said. "Look at the dogs. They're not acting so mad anymore, are they?"

Finished eating, the dogs now stood looking up at the girls, panting and licking their lips. One of them sniffed the empty bag, looked up again, and wagged its stump of a tail.

"What a couple of fakers!" Nancy said. "They aren't really attack dogs—they're just here to scare people away."

"And they do a great job," Bess remarked. "Come on, you guys, let's go."

But Nancy had already started climbing back down the wall, talking softly and holding out the back side of her hand for the dogs to sniff. "It's okay," she called to the other two. "They're not going to have us for dessert."

"I wouldn't be so sure of that," Bess said. But she followed George back down the wall and cautiously patted one of the dogs on the head. "The next time, I'll bring steak," she told the dog. It whined. "Uh-oh," she said. "I think he knows that word."

"Okay, let's go to the house," Nancy said. "These dogs might start barking again if they realize we're empty-handed."

Trailed by the dogs, Nancy, Bess, and George walked across the grounds until they came to the main door of Harrington House. It was huge, with brass hinges and a brass lion's-head knocker.

"I'm surprised there isn't an armed guard," George remarked. "This place looks like a fortress."

"I get the feeling I won't be able to break into this door very easily," Nancy agreed. "I might as well knock."

Nancy slammed the knocker three times. As she was raising it for the fourth time, the door was pulled open by a young man. Wearing faded jeans and a blue sweatshirt, he looked worried and busy, but he definitely didn't look threatening.

When he saw the girls, his frown disappeared. "Oh, great!" he said. "I was afraid you'd never get here."

"So were we," Bess told him.

"Well, come on in," he said, waving the manila folder he was holding. "I'll show you what to do."

As they followed him across a marble-floored entry hall the size of Nancy's living room, George whispered, "Who do you suppose he thinks we are?"

"I don't know," Nancy whispered back. "Let's play along and find out."

"Good idea," Bess said. "He's really cute."

The young man led them down another narrower hall and into a large room, whose walls were lined with books. Leather armchairs had been moved aside, and in the middle of the room was a long wooden table piled with papers and boxes of envelopes.

"There are coffee and doughnuts over there," he said, pointing to a smaller table by the fireplace. "So get comfortable and start stuffing."

"Start what?" Bess asked.

"Stuffing," he said. "You're volunteers, right? You're here to stuff campaign flyers?"

"That's right," Nancy said quickly.

"Good. My name's Barry, by the way," he told her. "I'm in charge until Todd and his manager get back. So if you have any questions, just ask. I'll be in the next room—that's where the phones are."

When Barry left the room, Nancy burst out laughing. "Sorry, you guys. If we stay here long enough, I'll figure out a way to get into that tower. I hope you don't mind stuffing a few envelopes."

"Just as long as I don't have to lick them," George said.

"I don't mind at all." Helping herself to a powdered-sugar doughnut, Bess sat down at the long table. "Barry's the best-looking guy I've seen all day!"

A few hours, two doughnuts, and hundreds of envelopes later, Nancy was beginning to wonder if she'd ever get out of that room. Barry kept popping his head in, making sure they were doing okay, but he never once suggested that they take a break. It wasn't really fair to keep Bess and George there so long, but since they hadn't complained yet, Nancy decided to give it another half hour.

Ten minutes later Barry stuck his head around the door again. "Still going strong, I see."

Bess stood up and stretched, giving him one of her brightest smiles. "We could go a lot stronger if we had a break, Barry. Don't you think the help deserves a little time off?"

Barry looked surprised. "Well, sure, no problem. In fact, I have some hero sandwiches in the other room. Care to join me?"

"That sounds great," Nancy told him, "but what we really need is a little exercise. Maybe we'll just take a walk around the grounds, if that's okay."

"Fine. But take a couple of doughnuts for the dogs," he said. "Feed them and they're your friends. Otherwise, they tend to hold a grudge."

After Barry left, Nancy counted to twenty. Then she left the library, followed by Bess and George. The three of them went down the hall, through what looked like a ballroom, and down another hall until they reached a back staircase. They took the stairs up to the third floor. At the end of a corridor was a narrow circular staircase.

"This has to be it," Nancy said. "Come on, let's get up to that tower room."

The door to John Harrington's tower office obviously hadn't been opened in a long time. Its hinges creaked as Nancy pushed it, and when they went in, a musty smell almost knocked them over.

"Whatever you're looking for, I hope you find it fast," Bess said, fanning the air. "I don't think I can breathe for long in here."

"What *are* you looking for, anyway?" George asked.

"I don't know," Nancy admitted. "Any clue. Something that will tell me what happened up here thirty years ago."

As she talked, Nancy moved around the office pulling dustcovers off the furniture. She opened the desk drawers, hoping something amazing would be there, but all she saw were papers, yellowed with age.

She was just about to give up when Bess called out. "Hey, look what I found!"

Turning, Nancy saw a panel in the wall slide open. She crossed the room and watched with Bess and George as a dumbwaiter rose creakily from the depths of the house.

"Really nice," George commented. "Whenever John Harrington got hungry, he just sent down to the kitchen for a snack."

"I should have known Harrington House would have one of these," Nancy said.

By sitting bent at the waist, Nancy could fit inside the dumbwaiter and almost be comfortable. After climbing back out, she pushed the button on the wall and sent the dumbwaiter slowly back down. Before closing the panel, Nancy stuck her head in the shaft and looked around. Along the inside of the wall she saw a bunch of wires that weren't connected to the dumbwaiter.

Nancy pushed the button again; the dumbwaiter started moving back up. Peering along the inside of the wall, Nancy saw that the wires led into the back of a black box. She pulled her head back in and walked down the room until she came to the spot on the wall where the box had to be.

"What is it, Nan?" Bess asked.

"I think it's a tape recorder!" Nancy said, running her fingers along the wall. "Feel."

The wall wasn't completely solid, and behind a canvas covering painted to look like the rest of the paneling, Bess and George could feel the outlines of an open-reel recorder.

"Weird," George said. "I wonder why he hid it."

"I was wondering exactly the same thing," Nancy told her.

"Maybe he liked music," Bess said, "but he didn't want to have to look at the machine. After all, those old ones weren't very pretty."

"Yes, but where are the tapes?" Nancy wondered. "I looked through all the drawers and cabinets. There's not a single tape anywhere."

"Somebody must have packed them away," George said.

Feeling along the wall again, Nancy found two more canvas coverings, smaller than the one for the tape recorder. "I'll bet these are speakers," she said. "If I win, you stuff the rest of my envelopes."

"You mean we're staying here?" Bess asked. "Sorry, Nan. Barry's cute, but I don't think I could stuff one more envelope. Not even for him."

Laughing, Nancy was just about to rip the canvas away from the wall when the office door was flung open.

A man was standing in the doorway. A tall, thin man who looked furious. He had a shotgun in his hands. It was pointed straight at Nancy.

Chapter

Nine

"WHAT ARE YOU doing in here?" the man growled, his voice deep and threatening. "This room is off-limits!" He waved his shotgun, motioning them toward the door. "Get out. Now, before I use this on you!"

"Wait just a minute," Nancy said. "Before we tell you who we are, why don't you tell us who you are?"

"I'm the caretaker—not that it's any of your business," he told her. "And my business is keeping trespassers off this property."

"Trespassers!" Bess tried to sound insulted. "For your information, we happen to be volunteers for Todd Harrington's campaign."

"Oh? Then what are you doing up here?" he asked.

"We didn't know where to go," Nancy told him, quickly making up the story. "The front door was open and nobody was here, so we just wandered around the house until we found this room." She took a few steps toward the man, staring at him angrily. "And let me tell you, if Mr. Harrington hears about this, he's not going to be happy. So why don't you stop pointing that gun at us and tell us where we're supposed to be?"

Slowly the man lowered the shotgun until it was pointing at the floor. He took a few steps back and then gestured toward the door. "Downstairs," he said. "You're supposed to be downstairs."

"Where downstairs?" Nancy asked. She had a funny feeling that this man wasn't the caretaker. "Third floor? Second floor? First?"

"Find it yourselves," the man said. "And don't come snooping up here again, or it'll be *you* Mr. Harrington'll be unhappy with."

Raising the gun again, the man backed out the door, slamming it behind him.

"Quick!" Nancy cried as soon as he was gone. "Let's follow him!"

"I thought you were interested in that tape recorder," Bess said.

"I am, but it'll have to wait." Nancy yanked

open the door. "Right now I'm more interested in finding out who that guy really is!"

His voice was different from the one in my garage, Nancy thought as they clattered down the winding stairs, but he's tall. And I'll bet he was the guy in my garage and the guy who followed me in that black car.

As they dashed down the big entry hall toward the front door, they almost collided with Barry. "What's the rush?" he said, looking startled.

"The caretaker!" Nancy shouted, without stopping. "Which way'd the caretaker go?"

"You mean old Al? It's Al's day off," Barry said. "Hey!" he called after them. "What about the envelopes?"

"Later!" Nancy called back. "Sorry!"

Outside, there was no sign of the "caretaker." Nancy stopped for a second and listened. There it was—the sound of a car, its engine roaring as it sped down the long drive toward the front gates.

"Come on!" Nancy cried. "If we hurry, we might just make it!"

Together, the three girls rushed across the grounds and through the trees, heading for the crumbled part of the wall they'd climbed earlier. If we can get to my car in time, Nancy thought, we can follow him all the way back to River Heights if we have to.

Just as they were scrambling over the wall, Nancy heard a car again. This time it was moving fast down the cliff road, but suddenly it stopped. The girls continued to run through the woods, following the wall out to the road. As they were just about to break through the last of the under-brush, they heard the car start up again and roar away.

They sprinted the couple hundred feet to the Mustang and piled in. Before the doors were even shut, Nancy was turning the key in the ignition.

But the engine didn't start. Instead, it groaned and clunked. Her hand shaking, Nancy tried again. Another groan and clunk, but still no life.

"Sounds as if the battery's dead," George said.

"It can't be." Fumbling with the door handle, Nancy got out of the car and raised the hood. "The battery's fine," she called out. "But that jerk just took my distributor cap!"

Slamming down the hood, Nancy shook her head in frustration. The shotgun-toting "care-taker" was probably halfway back to town by then.

Slowly this time, the girls trudged back to Harrington House. While Bess apologized to Barry for their running out on him, Nancy called for a tow truck. The truck took an hour to arrive, and when they finally got back to town, Nancy realized she wouldn't have time to go home and clean up for her meeting with Mayor Abbott.

"Actually, it's been kind of fun," Bess said as the three of them left the repair station in the fixed Mustang. "I even got some exercise, and it was a lot more exciting than jogging."

"I get the feeling your jogging days are over," George commented.

"Right," Bess agreed. "I just found a new interest—working for the Harrington campaign."

Laughing, Nancy let them out by a bus stop downtown, then parked and went into the mayor's outer office. She was tired, her clothes were dirty from climbing the wall, and her hair needed a good brushing, but at least she was on time.

Unfortunately, the mayor wasn't. "He's in an important meeting," his secretary explained to Nancy. "He'll be with you as soon as he can."

Forty-five minutes went by. Nancy jumped every time the secretary's intercom buzzed, and then slumped back in her chair, waiting. Finally, after an hour, the mayor emerged from his office.

"Sorry to keep you waiting, Miss Drew," Sam Abbott said, shaking her hand. His dark hair was graying, and he looked tired, but his blue eyes were clear and sharp. Nancy knew that he didn't miss a thing. "Come on in and let's talk."

Feeling very rumpled, Nancy went into the mayor's office and sat down in a soft leather chair. "I guess you know that I'm investigating John Harrington's death," she said.

"Yes, my secretary mentioned that," the mayor said, easing into the chair behind his shiny wooden desk. He studied her for a minute before continuing, "Do you really think you'll be able to uncover anything new—or that there is anything to uncover?"

Nancy started to say that since she'd been threatened three times already, she was pretty sure that somebody was trying to keep something covered up. But then she changed her mind. After all, she reasoned, she couldn't trust anybody—not even the mayor of River Heights.

"I don't really know," she answered. "But I'm going to try."

"Well, I wish you luck." The mayor smiled and leaned back in his chair. "Now, how can I help you?"

Even though she knew what he was going to say, Nancy asked him to tell her what had happened the night John Harrington died. And she was right—Mayor Abbott didn't tell her anything she hadn't already heard. Yes, Charles Ogden had asked for a raise. In fact, he—Abbott—had been there at the time. And, yes, Ogden had been upset when he left, but when he had come back he seemed calm.

"And later he drove you home?" Nancy asked.

"That's right. It was about eleven-thirty."

And John Harrington was killed sometime around midnight, Nancy thought. Ogden couldn't have gotten back in time to do it.

"What about Neil Gray?" she asked.

Neil Gray had been upset, too, the mayor told her. "In fact," he said, "*upset* isn't quite the word for it—*outraged* is better. The man ranted and raved in the entry hall, accusing John Harrington of sabotaging his campaign and ruining his life. I practically had to throw him out the door."

"You wouldn't happen to know where Neil Gray is, would you?" Nancy asked. "Or Charles Ogden?"

The mayor shook his head. "I'm afraid not, Miss Drew. But I wouldn't waste my time with Ogden, if I were you. For what it's worth, I'd put my money on Neil Gray. I suspected him then, and I suspect him now."

"Because of the way he acted?"

"Of course," the mayor agreed. "But it's more

than that." He leaned across the desk, his eyes serious and concerned. "Neil Gray had no chance running against John Harrington. Mr. Harrington was an outstanding man, and he was going to be the best governor this state ever had. Neil Gray knew it—and he couldn't stand it."

An outstanding man? Nancy wondered as she drove home ten minutes later. If John Harrington had been so outstanding, it must have been the best-kept secret in the state. Nancy's own father didn't think he'd been so outstanding. Ned's parents didn't think he should have been put up on a pedestal. Charles Ogden and Neil Gray presumably disliked him. So why did Mayor Abbott think he had been so terrific?

Of course, Sam Abbott had been John Harrington's personal secretary, Nancy reminded herself. He probably knew more about him than most people. Still, it was funny that the mayor was the only one who thought Harrington was one of the good guys.

When Nancy got home, every outside light was blazing even though it was barely dusk yet. Nancy had told Hannah what had happened the night before, and it was obvious that Hannah was making sure no one else sneaked into their garage.

Nancy parked her car in the driveway—just in case—then got out and headed for the front door. Max, the neighbors' black cat, was standing on the porch. Nancy stooped to pet him—and just then she heard a scream.

The scream was coming from inside her house, and the voice was Hannah's.

Chapter

Ten

"THIEF!" HANNAH SCREAMED, her terrified voice ringing through the night.

Before Nancy could move, the front door flew open and Hannah rushed outside, colliding with Nancy, who fell backward, stepping on Max's paw. Yowling and hissing, the cat took off like a streak.

"Hannah, what happened?" Nancy cried as she scrambled up.

"Inside!" Hannah gasped. "He's still inside!"

Without waiting to hear any more, Nancy ran into the house, skidding on the hall rug and almost falling into the living room. The room was a wreck, but no one was there.

Next she went into the den. It was a mess, too—the desk drawers had been pulled out and emptied, the couch pillows were tossed on the floor, books and records were scattered everywhere.

A soft thump from the kitchen made Nancy freeze. Then, cautiously, she tiptoed out of the den and down the hall. Her heart pounding, she peered into the kitchen.

Cereal boxes, cans, and cookbooks littered the floor. A bag of flour had been ripped open, vegetables and fruit were dumped in the sink, and the garbage can was turned upside down. The back door stood wide open, and in the doorway stood Max the cat.

Nancy let her breath out. It must have been the cat she had heard, and not the thief. Whoever had wrecked the house had escaped.

"Nancy?" A pale-faced Hannah appeared in the doorway. "Are you all right? Is he gone?"

Nancy nodded, heading for the phone to call the police. "What happened, Hannah?"

"I don't really know," Hannah said. "I was visiting next door. When I came back, I took one look at the kitchen and I knew we'd been robbed, but I didn't even think that the thief might still be here. I was walking toward the living room when I heard a noise coming from the den." She shuddered. "I got there just in time to see a man leaving by the front door."

On the phone, Nancy told the police what had happened, gave her name and address, and then turned back to Hannah. "What did he look like?" she asked.

"I'm afraid I couldn't see him," Hannah admitted. "I was terrified. And he was wearing dark clothes and dark leather gloves. And he had a ski mask over his entire head, like one of those international terrorists."

"A terrorist wouldn't waste his time with us. This guy was just a run-of-the-mill housebreaker." Nancy glanced around the kitchen. "I can't believe what a mess this place is. Maybe we should just move!"

A loud rapping at the front door sent the cat scurrying outside and made Hannah and Nancy jump. "It can't be our friendly visitor," Nancy said with a nervous laugh. "He wouldn't knock."

Two policemen stood on the porch, and Nancy let them in. "Get ready for a wreck," she told them as they followed her into the living room. She took them through the entire house and for the first time got a look at what the thief had done to her bedroom.

"It's going to take forever to put it back together," she moaned, staring at the papers, clothes, and cassette tapes that covered every inch of the floor.

"Yep," one of the officers agreed cheerfully. "The guy didn't miss much, I've got to hand him that."

I'd like to hand him something, Nancy thought, looking around her room. A broom, for one. And a prison uniform.

While the police were questioning Hannah in the kitchen, Nancy halfheartedly picked up a pile of cassettes and stacked them on top of her recorder. She gathered an armful of sweaters from the floor and started toward the dresser. Suddenly she let the bright-colored tops slip back out of her hands.

What had the policeman said—that the guy didn't miss much? But her tape recorder was still there, in plain sight on the white Formica shelf. Next to it was her television, and on the desk sat a personal computer. If Nancy had been out doing a dishonest day's work, she wouldn't have passed those up.

And what about the TV and the stereo and the VCR downstairs?

Frowning, Nancy went back through those rooms and saw what she'd missed before—nothing valuable was gone. In fact, it didn't look as though anything was gone. She walked into the kitchen, found the extra sugar bowl they used for change, and opened it. Coins and a few dollar bills were still inside.

"He wouldn't be after the small change," one of the policemen pointed out.

Nancy nodded. "But he wasn't after the big change, either. I just noticed, he didn't take anything he could sell, like the TV or my tape recorder."

"Yeah, I noticed that, too," the officer agreed. "Weird thief, huh?"

"I'm pretty sure he wasn't a thief at all," Nancy told him. "I think this whole thing was just a way of trying to scare me." Quickly she explained about her investigation into John Harrington's death and the other warnings she'd gotten.

"And you think that's what this was?" the policeman asked. "Another warning?"

"I'm positive."

He gave a low whistle. "Well, you may be right. And if you are, maybe you ought to back off. This guy sounds serious."

"He is," Nancy said, walking with them to the door. "But so am I. And I'm not about to back off."

Wishing her luck, the policemen headed for

their car. Nancy was just about to close the door when she saw a car pull up. Ned got out and walked toward her.

He couldn't have come at a worse time, Nancy thought, trying to comb her hair with her fingers. I look as if I've been on a five-day hike.

"What's going on?" Ned asked, a worried look in his brown eyes. "Why were the police here? Are you all right?"

"*I* am," Nancy said. "But the house may never be the same." She sat down on the front steps and told Ned what had happened.

Shaking his head, Ned sat down beside her. "What are you going to do?"

"What can I do but solve the case as fast as I can," Nancy said. She leaned back against a porch pillar and closed her eyes. "I just wish I had something more to go on. So far, I don't have a single good lead." As Nancy spoke, Max leaped silently onto the porch and rubbed against her ankles. Nancy scratched him between the ears until he purred.

"He likes you," Ned said.

"Umm."

"So do I."

Nancy looked over and smiled at Ned. "The feeling's mutual," she said softly. Maybe the day wouldn't be a total loss after all.

Ned scooted a little closer to her. "I came by to see if you wanted to go for a ride, maybe get something to eat," he said. "I tried to call, but your phone wasn't working."

"It wasn't? It worked fine when I called the police."

Ned shrugged. "I don't know. Must have just been something temporary. Anyway, how about supper?"

"Supper sounds great." It really does, Nancy thought. She just wished she could go. "But even if the house could clean itself, I couldn't leave Hannah," she explained. "Seeing that guy really shook her up."

Ned nodded, and Nancy was glad to see that he looked sympathetic. "And I'd invite you in, but we'd have to do a major clean-up before we could even sit down," she said.

"It's okay," Ned told her. "It's nice out here." He scooted closer to Nancy. "A front porch is always a good place for a nice serious talk."

Serious? Suddenly Nancy was worried. What was he going to say? She swallowed and sat up straighter, trying to get ready for whatever Ned had to tell her.

"Nancy," he said, reaching for her hand, "this is really hard—"

At that moment Hannah opened the front door.

Normally she would have gone back inside to give them privacy. But right then Hannah hardly seemed to notice that Ned was there. She looked worried, nervous—and determined.

"Nancy, I have to talk to you," she said. "It's very important."

"Sure, Hannah," Nancy said, wondering what could be wrong. She turned to Ned to apologize, but he'd already stood up.

"I'll talk to you later," he said.

"Okay," Nancy said. She was almost relieved. After all, if Ned was going to give her bad news, she could wait to hear it. Right then she was more worried about Hannah.

"I've never spoken to anyone about this," Hannah said after they stepped back inside and went into the kitchen. "For years I kept it a secret, and after all this time I started to think it was all just my imagination. But I can't think that anymore." She took a deep breath. "This case you're on could be dangerous, Nancy, and I have to tell you what I've kept secret all this time."

Nancy couldn't imagine Hannah having any kind of horrible secret. "What is it?" she asked.

Hannah clasped her hands together nervously, but her voice was steady. "I've always thought— and I still think—that Charlie Ogden might have killed John Harrington."

98

Chapter

Eleven

COMPLETELY STUNNED, NANCY stared at Hannah. Of course, Nancy herself had thought that Charles Ogden might have been involved in John Harrington's death. But to hear Hannah—who'd been in love with the man—say that he might be a murderer was a real jolt.

"I wasn't completely honest with you, Nancy," Hannah went on. "I told you that Charlie was upset when he didn't get that raise. But the truth is, he was absolutely furious. And when he left, he told me he was going to go back and give Mr. Harrington a piece of his mind." Hannah shook her head. "I'd never seen Charlie like that; he was so angry it was frightening."

"But you calmed him down," Nancy reminded her. "Mayor Abbott said he was okay when he came back. Besides, Hannah, Ogden's and the mayor's stories match. They left Harrington House together, and John Harrington was still alive then."

"Yes, I know all that," Hannah agreed. "But I haven't told you the worst part yet."

Even though she felt bad for Hannah, Nancy couldn't help being excited. This could be her first break on the case. "What is it?" she asked.

"After John Harrington died, Charlie acted very strangely," Hannah said. "Oh, he didn't pretend to be broken up over Mr. Harrington's death, and I guess after the way he'd been treated, that wasn't hard to understand."

"Then what was strange about the way he acted?"

"He was nervous and excited," Hannah explained. "As if he had a secret he couldn't tell. And he said he'd come up with a way to get enough money so that we could get married."

"That doesn't sound so awful," Nancy said.

"No, but whenever I asked how he was going to get the money, he wouldn't tell me," Hannah said. "He just said it looked like a sure thing."

"And you believed him?"

"I didn't know what to believe. I thought I was

in love with him, but he was acting so differently. He'd always been so open, and now he was quiet, secretive." Hannah looked as if she might start to cry. After a moment she said, "Charlie told me that if his plan worked, he might have to leave town for a while. He told me not to worry—that he'd come back for me." She turned to face Nancy, her eyes bright with tears. "But," she said softly, "he never came back."

Nancy felt terrible. She knew what Hannah was saying—that Charles Ogden killed John Harrington, helped himself to some money from his estate, then waited until the police investigation was over and skipped town to start a new life, leaving Hannah behind.

Could he really have done it? Nancy wondered. The police reports had said that no money was missing, but there could have been some stashed away—in a place only a few people, including the chauffeur, knew about.

But even if it had happened that way, Nancy couldn't prove it. Not unless someone could point a finger at Charles Ogden. Hannah was suspicious, but suspicions didn't count. Nancy needed proof, and she didn't have it. Besides, nobody seemed to know where Ogden was, and if Nancy couldn't find him, she knew she was right back where she'd started.

"I'm glad you told me, Hannah," she said softly. "I know how hard this must have been on you."

Hannah was calmer then. "It took a long time for me to accept that Charlie had run out on me," she said. "But even before he left, I realized I hadn't known him as well as I thought. He'd changed in those last few days into a person I wasn't sure I wanted to marry. So maybe it was just as well that he ran off." She sighed, but smiled at Nancy.

Nancy gave her a hug. "Why don't you relax for the rest of the night? I'll clean up."

But Hannah refused to let Nancy do all the work. Together, they straightened up the mess the "thief" had made. It took four hours, and by the time they'd finished, Nancy fell into bed, expecting to be asleep instantly.

Instead, she found herself wide-awake, her head full of questions that she couldn't answer. Had Charles Ogden murdered John Harrington? He could have, but when? He had driven Sam Abbott home around eleven-thirty, so how had he gotten back in time to kill Harrington at midnight?

Nancy sat up in bed and flipped her pillow over, trying to get more comfortable. Of course, she thought, the times might not be completely exact.

Ogden and Abbott could have left at ten-thirty, and that would have given Ogden time to get back. The only problem was that Mayor Abbott had been so sure that it was eleven-thirty.

Sitting up again, Nancy kicked back the light-weight quilt, got up and opened her window more, then flopped back down on the bed. She wasn't sure if Hannah's suspicions were worth worrying about. Charles Ogden might have acted strangely, but that didn't make him a killer. Nancy thought he sounded more like a creep. Maybe he had found a little Harrington money hidden somewhere, and then skipped town with it. If that was true, then Hannah was better off without him.

And what about Neil Gray? she wondered, bunching her pillow underneath her head. So far, he was still her best suspect. He'd been raving, according to Mayor Abbott. And even though his appointment had been canceled, he could have hidden somewhere and then killed Harrington after everyone else had left. He had had the best motive—John Harrington was ruining his campaign and reputation and he wanted revenge.

And, Nancy told herself, turning onto her stomach and shoving her pillow onto the floor, you don't know where Neil Gray is, either.

Nancy got up and went into the bathroom for a drink of water. Think about something else, she told herself so she would relax and get to sleep. Think about some*one* else.

Unfortunately, the only other person who came to mind was Ned. And thoughts of Ned—and that "serious" talk he'd wanted to have—didn't lull her to sleep either. Nancy tossed and turned for at least another hour, wondering if Ned was about to call their relationship off.

She was awakened by her bedside phone ringing. Nancy grabbed the phone. "Ned?"

"Hardly," Brenda Carlton said. "But now I know where your mind is. No wonder you haven't solved this case yet."

Bleary eyed, Nancy looked at her alarm clock. "Eight-thirty?" she grumbled. "I hope you didn't call me up at eight-thirty in the morning just for fun, Brenda."

"What's that noise?" Brenda asked.

"What noise?"

"It's a clicking. You sound like a record that's skipping," Brenda complained.

Nancy heard it then, too, but she didn't care what it was. "Forget it," she said. "It's a lousy connection. Why don't you just tell me why you called?"

Brenda gave a throaty little laugh. "I called

because I thought you ought to be the first to know—I've solved the case."

Suddenly wide awake, Nancy sat straight up. "You've what? I don't believe it."

"What's the matter?" Brenda asked. "Are you jealous?"

Nancy yawned loudly. "No, I'm just being realistic. You couldn't have solved it, Brenda. There's not enough to go on."

"That's what you think," Brenda retorted.

"Okay, so tell me."

"Oh, no! You'll have to read it in the *Times* with everyone else."

"Brenda, you can't write a story without concrete proof and without a murderer. It would be all speculation. You have to tie up all the loose ends and deliver the criminal to the police."

"Well, maybe I can tell you first. But not on the phone; we'll meet later. And maybe you could wrap up all the teeny-tiny little details for me. Actually, it would be good to tell you. You might learn something about investigative technique from me. Oh, excuse me, I don't mean to gloat, Nancy, but you haven't been doing your homework. But if I give you my information later, you'll have to promise not to act on it until I can write my story. That's the only way I'll tell what I've learned."

"Oh, Brenda, you're just plain—" Nancy just stopped herself from telling Brenda that she was silly. "All right, it's a deal," she said, swallowing her pride.

Forty-five minutes later Nancy pulled the Mustang into a parking space and got out. It was in a neglected section of town that was deserted even at nine-thirty in the morning. The kind of area with shadowy alleys, run-down buildings, and small shops with metal grates stretched across their entrances at night.

Brenda had told her to walk three blocks, turn right, and keep walking until she came to a bus stop. Nancy thought the whole meeting was absolutely ridiculous, like something out of a bad spy movie, but Brenda had insisted, she said, so that no one would follow them. Why they couldn't just have met in Brenda's office Nancy would never understand. Brenda got so carried away with the melodrama of the situation!

Nancy walked quickly. She wanted to hear the story and then get out of that neighborhood. She'd been there five minutes, and as far as she was concerned, that was five minutes too many.

Up ahead, Nancy saw the street where she was supposed to make a right turn. This better be a good story, she thought, picking up her pace.

It was hard to believe that Brenda had actually solved the case, but anything was possible. Well, at least Nancy would finally have the answers. She walked even faster, eager now to get to Brenda and hear what she had to say.

She was just about to turn the corner when she heard the sound. A scratchy, scraping sound, coming from the top of the four-story building beside her. Glancing up, Nancy saw movement—it looked like someone's hands and head sticking over the edge of the building for a second. But she didn't have time to observe closely because next to the disembodied person something was starting to teeter at the corner of the building.

It was a column of stone—a decorative element. As Nancy watched, it continued to wobble and then it started to fall—straight at her head.

Chapter

Twelve

MOVE! NANCY TOLD herself. Her body felt as if it were under water, but somehow she managed to leap forward, grazing her shoulder on the corner of the building.

She fell hard, scraping her hands on the rough pavement. The stone crashed onto the sidewalk behind her, breaking into pieces as if it were an eggshell. It landed where Nancy had been standing only seconds before. If it had hit her, she knew she would have been killed instantly.

I'll have to talk to Mayor Abbott, Nancy thought as she got shakily to her feet. This part of town is coming apart at the seams! But as she gently brushed off her scratched palms, she remembered the person she'd thought she had seen. Maybe it wasn't an accident. Maybe it was more of the same—someone trying to scare her off. And if it was, then things had just become very serious.

Stepping out into the middle of the street, Nancy craned her neck, trying to see if she could spot anyone up on the roof. All she saw was the gap where the stone decoration had been.

"Why are you here? I told you to meet me at the bus stop." Brenda Carlton's voice grated on Nancy.

Dressed in tight black pants and an oversize blouse, with a gold chain belt around her hips, Brenda strode impatiently down the street. But Nancy didn't look at her. She was running to the fire escape that ran down the side of the building. "You may have solved this case, Brenda," she said, "and I know you can't wait to gloat about it, but we have something more important to do first."

"We do? What?"

Nancy grabbed the rusted bottom rung and swung herself up. "Come on," she called back to Brenda. "We have to hurry!"

Nancy was wearing a soft purple running outfit, which made it easy for her to climb. But Brenda's clothes weren't good for much but sitting and standing. Sighing loudly, she heaved herself clumsily onto the fire escape steps. The thin high heel on one of her shoes immediately caught on the step and broke off. By this time, Nancy was halfway up the side of the building.

"Do you mind telling me what we're doing?" Brenda screeched, pulling off her shoe and stamping her bare foot.

"We're trying to find whoever just tried to kill me!" Nancy shouted back. "Hurry!"

The rest of the way up, Nancy could hear Brenda shrieking at her, but there was no time to answer. It might not be too late, she thought. The stone had fallen only a couple of minutes before.

The roof of the building was covered with black tarlike stuff that felt soft and gooey underfoot. In the middle of it was a high square shed with a door on one side. Except for that door, and a couple of metal bubbles that Nancy figured were for ventilation, the roof was empty. The roof of the next building was too far away to jump to safely, and the only way off the roof was the fire escape.

Cautiously, Nancy crept to the door that led into the building. She moved silently around one corner, then the next, and the next, ready to jump on anyone who might be hiding. No one was there. Quietly she tested the handle. It turned easily, and Nancy found herself staring down a steep stairway that led to the top floor of the building.

The building was four stories high, Nancy remembered. And her stone pusher could be hiding on any one of them. Her heart pounding, she put one foot on the top step and was peering down into the shadowy stairwell when she heard a noise behind her.

Nancy whirled around to see Brenda climbing clumsily off the fire escape and onto the tarry roof. Brenda's mouth was open, ready to complain again, but Nancy quickly put a finger to her lips and motioned her over.

Carrying her broken shoe, Brenda limped to the doorway. "I wish—"

"Ssh!" Nancy hissed. "Later! Now take off that other shoe and come on!"

Together Nancy and Brenda made their way down the first flight of stairs to the door leading into the fourth floor. It was locked. So was the door on the third floor. Finally, on the second floor, the door opened.

"Why didn't you just break into those other doors?" Brenda whispered.

"Because I figured the guy who wanted to kill me didn't have time to do it himself," Nancy whispered back. "He just tried to bash my head in, so he's not going to stand around picking locks. He wants an easy way out."

Brenda looked terrified. "So you think he might still be hiding in here? Why wouldn't he just take these stairs to the outside?"

"Because these will only go into the basement, and he wouldn't be able to get out. He had to go onto a floor and then take the inside stairs to the first floor, or he could have then taken the fire escape back down after we were off it. I am hoping that we'll surprise him and that he won't have left yet."

Nancy tiptoed quietly through the long hallway that was lined with doors. They must have been offices once, but she couldn't imagine anyone doing business there now. The hall was littered with trash, the tiles were broken, and cobwebs hung from the ceilings.

"You go that way around that corner and try doors," she told Brenda. "If one of the doors opens, don't go in. Just come get me."

Brenda put her hand nervously on a doorknob. It wouldn't turn. Satisfied that Brenda was at least going to try, Nancy was going around the corner when she heard Brenda scream.

Her hands over her mouth, her eyes wide with terror, Brenda stood in an open doorway. "I saw it!" she shrieked. "A rat! A huge, disgusting rat!"

With a sigh Nancy stepped into the room. It was small, with broken chairs and a battered desk. The floor was covered with a film of dust, and in the dust was a clear set of footprints leading to an open window. Through the window, Nancy could see the fire escape.

He's gone, she thought, looking down at the deserted street. And the only clue he left behind was his big, fat footprints. Checking the prints again, she saw that they really were big. They belonged to a tall man, probably, just like the one in the black car and the one in John Harrington's office—the one who wanted to do more than scare her.

"Nancy?" Brenda said nervously.

"It's okay," Nancy said, going into the hallway. "The rat's gone. Both of them. Come on, let's get out of here. This place gives me the creeps."

Back on the street, Nancy finally remembered why Brenda had asked her there. "Okay, Brenda," she said. "I have to admit it'll make me jealous, but if you really have solved the case, at least it'll be over. So tell me."

"Well." Brenda smiled importantly. "It just so happens that I found Neil Gray."

Nancy's mouth dropped open. "And he confessed to killing John Harrington?"

"Not yet," Brenda told her. "But I'm sure he

will once the police take him into custody. What he *did* confess was that he took that shot at Todd the other day."

"Where is he?" Nancy asked.

"Oh, no! *I* found him, and he's mine," Brenda said. "But I will tell you this—he's changed his name, and he's become almost a hermit, living alone and brooding about the Harringtons. He absolutely despises them," she went on. "He said that when he found out about Todd's campaign, he didn't know what came over him. It was as though all the awful stuff that's been haunting him had come alive again! Isn't that fantastic?"

Nancy nodded. "But he didn't admit to killing Todd's father?"

"No, he just told the same old story—that his appointment had been canceled and he went home without ever seeing John Harrington. But as I said, once the police get him, I bet he'll talk!"

Nancy wasn't so sure, but she didn't want to argue. "Is he tall?" she asked, suddenly wondering if Neil Gray and the tall, skinny man with the shotgun were the same person.

"Six feet, at least!"

Very slowly then Nancy asked her to describe the man. After hearing Brenda's description, Nancy knew her tall, skinny man was not Neil Gray. She had been hoping that he had been following her and also that he was the killer of John Harrington.

If he wasn't Gray, she thought, then who was he? Charles Ogden? No, Ogden was only about five feet five. Therefore, the skinny man had to be a hired accomplice, Nancy reasoned, and anyone could have hired him. She was no further along than she had been, except that now she knew that Neil Gray was not following her.

Nancy started to think more about the man who had pushed the stone over. How had he known to wait for her on the roof of that particular building that morning? She hadn't been followed, she was sure of that. In spite of the sun, Nancy shivered. How had he known?

Chapter

Thirteen

As she followed Brenda's flashy red car out of the run-down section of town a few minutes later, Nancy had an overwhelming urge to keep on following her. After all—unbelievable as it seemed—Brenda had found Neil Gray. And Nancy would have given almost anything to talk to the man. She knew she could find out more from him than Brenda had.

Unfortunately, Brenda turned down the street the newspaper office was on, and Nancy had no choice but to keep on driving.

All right, admit it, she told herself as she headed home, you're jealous. Brenda found Neil

116

Gray and you didn't. She beat you on that one, and you don't like it one bit.

But had Brenda beaten Nancy on the really important one? Had Neil Gray killed John Harrington?

He hated the Harringtons, Nancy thought; he hadn't bothered to keep that a secret. And he'd admitted shooting at Todd, which hardly helped his case any. Somehow, though, Nancy had trouble believing that a man who was so honest about the way he felt would bother hiding what he'd done—even if what he'd done was murder. Neil Gray was so down on the Harringtons that he probably would have bragged about killing one of them. And it wasn't just jealousy that made her want to solve this case. It was not knowing what had happened that was driving her crazy.

By the time Nancy got home, the morning sun had been covered by a blanket of gray clouds, and a light rain was falling. After she let herself in through the back door of the house, she grabbed an apple from the kitchen table and headed for her room. The phone rang and she stopped to pick it up in the den.

"Hi," Ned said.

Nancy's mood suddenly turned gray, too. Was Ned going to tell her everything was over between them? That was all she needed. "Hi," she answered. She almost wished she'd missed his call.

"How's everything?" he asked. "The house back together again?"

"Just about." The connection was still lousy, and Nancy reminded herself to complain to the phone company. Then, hoping to keep Ned from saying whatever he wanted to say, she started talking fast, telling him about Brenda and Neil Gray and the stone that had just missed crushing her skull.

"This is getting serious," Ned said.

"Everyone keeps telling me that, and I'm beginning to believe it."

"It's true," Ned told her. "Listen, Nancy, about last night. I wanted to—"

"You know what I think I'm going to do?" Nancy said, interrupting. "I think I'll go back to Harrington House. There's something I want to check out, and Todd's going to be back soon, so I might not have another chance." Anything, she thought. Anything to keep Ned from giving her bad news.

"Okay," Ned said doubtfully. "But be careful, Nancy. I mean it. You don't know what's going on, and you could get hurt."

"You're right," Nancy agreed. At least he still

cares about whether or not I get hurt, she thought. "But don't worry. I'll be careful."

"Call me when you get back," Ned suggested. "I'd like to know what you find out, and besides, I really want to talk to you."

Nancy wasn't so sure she really wanted to talk to him, but she agreed to call when she got back. Still eating the apple, she went back to the kitchen, grabbed a couple of slices of ham from the refrigerator, got back in the Mustang, and headed for Harrington House. She'd used it as an excuse to put Ned off, and she still wasn't sure what she was looking for, but anything was better than sitting at home.

After she parked in the narrow turnaround, Nancy got out and followed the wall to the broken spot. As soon as she touched down on the other side, the dogs came tearing toward her. But this time she was prepared. "Here, you moochers," she called, tossing the ham at them. Satisfied, the dogs ignored her as she sprinted toward the mansion.

Nancy decided to try to sneak past Barry. If she didn't, she'd wind up stuffing a thousand envelopes, and she definitely was not in the mood for that.

The front door was unlocked. Nancy let herself

in, then tiptoed past the campaign rooms and up the circular staircase.

The minute Nancy entered John Harrington's office, she knew what she wanted to see: that tape recorder, hidden behind the canvas panel. Had Todd's father been a music freak? And if so, where were his tapes?

Nancy tried to lock the office door, but the lock didn't work. The best she could do was shut it tightly. She located the canvas panel and managed to scrape a corner of it loose. Then, using her fingernails, she ripped and tugged until the canvas pulled free, showering the dusty Oriental carpet with chips and slivers of paint.

A tape was still on one of the reels, its loose end dangling free. Hoping that it wouldn't fall apart in her hands, Nancy carefully fed it onto the other reel. Then, crossing her fingers that it still worked, she checked to see that it was plugged in and then pushed the power button. A small red light came on. Nancy pushed Rewind. As if it had been waiting for someone to put it into action, the machine clicked and whirred, the tape rolling smoothly from one reel to the other.

When the tape was rewound, Nancy pushed Play and stood back to listen.

"But, John," a man said in a shaken voice, "I don't understand!"

"Oh, I think you do," another man said. His voice was smooth and steady, the voice of a man completely in charge. "You came to me and asked to be part of my staff. No one else would hire you because of your reputation, but I said yes even though you were suspected of buying votes in the last election."

"But I told you I wouldn't do it anymore. And now you're asking me to break the law again? You want me to go out and buy votes for *you*."

"No. I'm not *asking* you," the second voice said. "I'm *telling* you. Because if you don't, I'll see to it that you are prosecuted for your mistakes, and you'll never work in this state again!"

Silence followed. Nancy listened to the soft hiss of the tape and shook her head in disbelief. Whether Neil Gray had killed Harrington or not, she thought, he was right about him—John Harrington was *not* one of the good guys. What she had just heard was blackmail. She tensed as another voice came through the speakers. Was she going to hear more of the same?

It was just some quiet chatter between John Harrington and a speech writer. Then another period of silence, followed by a ringing telephone. John Harrington murmured softly and listened a lot, and Nancy had no idea what the conversation was about.

Finally someone else joined him, and as Nancy listened, she realized it was Charles Ogden, the chauffeur.

"Yes, Charles?" Harrington snapped.

"Sorry to disturb you, sir," Ogden said. "I wanted to let you know that I had those repairs taken care of. The limousine is in tip-top shape now."

"Let's hope so." A short pause. "Well?"

Charles Ogden cleared his throat. "Sir, I realize you're busy, but I need to speak to you about something personal."

Harrington sighed. "All right. What is it?"

"It's about my raise, sir," Ogden said. "I've been here a year now."

"A year? That long?"

"Yes, and you told me that, uh, after a year I'd probably get a raise."

"Hmm." There was a creak. Harrington probably leaned back in his chair, Nancy thought. "Yes, I remember saying that," he agreed. "But I also said that you'd probably get a raise *if* your work was satisfactory."

"Yes, you did," Ogden said.

"Sorry, Charles," Harrington said, not sounding sorry at all. "No raise."

"But, sir!"

"You don't really expect one, do you? After all

that has happened—cars breaking down, not ready on time, picking me up late—"

"But that one time I was late there was a traffic accident! I had to wait!"

"You should have left earlier," Harrington told him. His voice was cold now, the way it had been with the unlucky vote-buyer. "And just yesterday, you got a flat tire and I was twenty minutes late for a speech."

"Sir, cars do break down!" Charles Ogden sounded desperate now, and Nancy couldn't blame him. "None of the breakdowns have been my fault. You have to realize that!"

"I don't have to realize anything," Harrington said. "I think that's enough, Charles. It's late, and I've got work to do."

Nancy heard the slam of a door. Charles Ogden must have left without another word. Nancy was picturing him storming over to Hannah's, humiliated and angry, when suddenly it hit her. This conversation had been recorded on the day John Harrington died! She was actually listening to the man talk only a few hours before his death. And if she kept listening, she just might hear something that would unlock this whole mystery!

Impatiently pacing the office floor, Nancy waited for what seemed like forever. First Harrington's speech writer again, and a long conversation about what the main points of the speech were to be and where the jokes were to be inserted. The speech, Nancy noticed, made Harrington sound as though he cared more about the state and its people than anybody else in the world. *That's* the joke, she thought.

There wasn't a lot of tape left. As Nancy watched the rain come down outside, she wondered if the tape was going to be another dead end.

Finally, after a few more telephone calls, Nancy heard someone else come into the office. "I'm glad you're here," John Harrington said. "Because we have to have a talk, Sam."

Sam? He must be talking to Sam Abbott, once Harrington's personal secretary and now the mayor of River Heights!

Chapter

Fourteen

I'VE GOT THOSE reports you wanted," a younger-voiced Abbott said. "It's late, but I'll be glad to go over them with you now."

"Forget the reports for the moment," Harrington said. "Have a seat, Sam. We've both been so busy we haven't had a chance to talk lately."

Nancy heard another creak and figured that Abbott had sat down. "I have to admit, I'll be glad when the campaign's over," the future mayor said. "We could all use a couple weeks rest."

"Where are you planning to go?" Harrington asked.

Abbott chuckled. "I haven't had time to think

about it. Some friends have a house in the country —maybe I'll go there."

"Sounds nice," Harrington agreed. "But I'm surprised you don't just get yourself your own place. Or maybe do some traveling—Hawaii would be good this time of year, or the Caribbean."

"They'd be great," Abbott said, laughing. "But I'm afraid my wallet isn't fat enough for an island vacation."

"It's not?" Harrington sounded surprised. "I was sure you were carrying two wallets these days. One with your money in it, and the other filled with mine."

For a moment, neither man spoke. John Harrington had just accused Abbott of stealing from him, and Nancy held her breath, wondering what Abbott's answer would be.

Finally Abbott said, "Why do you say that?"

"I've watched you carefully, Sam," Harrington told him. "You're ambitious. You want power. The same kind of power I'll have as soon as I win the election."

"You haven't answered my question," Abbott reminded him. "Why do you think I've got a wallet stuffed with your money?"

"A conversation I overheard," Harrington answered. "Several conversations, as a matter of fact. I won't go into them all because they're all pretty much the same. In one you were talking to a stockbroker, and you were telling him where to invest the money you'd just 'inherited.'" Harrington laughed softly. "Now, I happen to know you never inherited any money, so I wondered where it came from. That's when I checked the books—my campaign fund books. You did a good job of covering up all the funds you embezzled," he said. "In fact, I doubt if anyone else could have spotted it."

"Then it can't be proven," Abbott said calmly.

"But you forgot—I overheard your conversations, Sam," Harrington said. "I have typed copies of them right here in the desk. You shouldn't have used this phone, you know. That was your biggest mistake."

Abbott still sounded calm. "This phone isn't tapped," he said. "You know it and I know it. You're bluffing."

"You're right about the phone not being tapped," Harrington agreed. "But listen to this." There was the sound of a drawer opening, and then he began reading. After listening for a minute, Nancy knew he wasn't bluffing.

Sam Abbott knew it, too. No longer calm, his

voice was tight and angry. "Where did you . . . how . . . ? What did you do, hide behind the bookcase and write down everything I said?"

No, Nancy thought. He had his hidden tape recorder going.

"Does it really matter?" Harrington asked. "The point is, I know what you've been up to. Now, I suppose you want to know what I'm going to do about it."

Abbott didn't say anything.

"I'm not going to fire you," Harrington said. "And I'm not going to turn you in. Of course, I do expect you to give the money back."

"That's all?" Abbott asked sarcastically.

"That's all," Harrington said. "Except that you'll never work for anyone but me, of course. And you'll never be free to be a political force on your own." He laughed again, a harsh, grating laugh. "From now on, you'll do exactly as I say."

"You can't do this!" Abbott cried angrily. "If you think I'm going to be your slave for the rest of my life, you're wrong!"

"Oh? What choice do you have?" Harrington asked. "Come on, Sam, you don't have *any* choice and you know it. You work for me, and you're always going to work for me."

Harrington laughed again. Then there was a

cry, a shout, and a crash. Frozen, Nancy listened to the sound of papers being ripped—and then the tape ran out, stopping with a click that made her jump.

Slowly Nancy went to the tape recorder and took off the reel of tape. Her hands were shaking. She had just heard Sam Abbott hit John Harrington, and even though she hadn't heard the rest, she could imagine what had happened. Abbott must have found every piece of evidence about himself in the desk, destroyed them all, and then thrown Harrington's body out the window.

But he didn't destroy all the evidence, Nancy thought, holding the tape. Because he didn't know about the most incriminating piece. Only John Harrington knew about his secret taping system, and if she hadn't stuck her head into that dumbwaiter shaft, she might never have found it, either.

Still stunned by what she'd heard, Nancy began searching through the desk drawers until she found an old manila envelope. Carefully she slipped the tape inside. You can't let anything happen to this, she told herself. It's the only proof you've got.

Nancy sealed the envelope and moved from behind the desk, planning to go downstairs to use one of Barry's phones to call the police. As she passed one window, she stopped for a minute and rested her hands on the windowsill, thinking and staring blankly past the sheets of water.

It was raining harder now. The wind was ripping leaves from the trees and splattering them against the pane. As she leaned forward, she looked far to her left and saw through the driving rain a black car pull up and stop beside the house.

It has to be the same one, she thought. But no one followed me here, so how did anyone know where I was? Was it just a lucky guess? No! Suddenly Nancy knew what had happened. No one had followed her there, and no one had followed her that morning when she went to meet Brenda. They don't need to follow me anymore, she thought. Because they tapped my phone! *That's* what that break-in was all about. It wasn't to scare me, it was to find out what I knew. They didn't take anything from my house—they added something. Bugs for the phones.

And Nancy knew then who'd ordered the break-in and the tap, too. Mayor Abbott. From the minute she'd started on this case, he'd been one step ahead of her, watching and waiting to see if she'd discover anything. Remembering the tall, skinny man she'd seen in his office the day she made her appointment, Nancy realized that he was the same guy who had held the shotgun on her and had tried to scare her off and kill her. And now the mayor had sent him after her again.

But he's out of luck, Nancy thought, heading for the door. He hasn't scared me off yet, and I'm not about to be killed. Not when I've got the evidence in my hands.

Nancy opened the door and raced for the circular staircase. She'd go down one floor, she thought, find a room, and hide in it until the mayor's lackey was gone. Then she'd get out of Harrington House and to the police as fast as she could.

Halfway down the spiral stairs, Nancy heard footsteps rushing down the hallway on the floor below. Silently she bounded back up and ran into the tower office and shut the door.

The footsteps were on the spiral stairs leading to the tower office now, and as Nancy looked frantically around the office, she realized that there was no place to hide.

Chapter

Fifteen

THE ONLY THING to do, Nancy thought, is to stand behind the door and rush out when it's opened. She flattened herself against the wall, her eyes still darting around the room. That was when she saw the button for the dumbwaiter.

In a second Nancy was across the room—jabbing at the button, listening to the footsteps on the stairs, and praying.

Outside the door, the footsteps slowed to a cautious walk. That was all the time Nancy needed. The dumbwaiter arrived, and she scrambled inside, jabbing the button just as the office door swung open.

As the dumbwaiter started to creak its way

down, Nancy heard the office door slam. Quick footsteps moved straight for the exposed tape recorder. Soon Mayor Abbott would figure out exactly how John Harrington had discovered what he was up to. But that won't help him any, Nancy thought, holding tightly to the crucial tape. He'll never get his hands on *this*.

It was dark and stuffy inside the dumbwaiter, but even in there Nancy could hear the thunder outside. The storm was getting worse. Driving down the cliff road in the middle of an electrical storm was not going to be fun, but Nancy knew she'd have to do it—and she'd have to do it quickly.

Finally, with a jerk and a thump, the dumbwaiter landed and Nancy slid the panel open. She got out and found herself in the biggest kitchen she'd ever seen. Two massive stoves were against one wall, and two refrigerators loomed against another. In the middle of the black- and white-tiled floor was a big wooden counter with copper pots and pans hanging over it.

The kitchen was dim, and the refrigerators and pans threw long shadows across the walls and floor. Tucking the tape into the waistband of her running pants, Nancy headed for a door. She'd almost reached it when she saw another shadow— the shadow of a man, hiding just beyond the door.

Nancy stopped. Mayor Abbott must really be worried, she thought. He'd sent two men after her. Looking around, she spotted another door, one she guessed that probably led up to the rest of the house. She turned quickly and started for it.

When she was halfway across the kitchen, the tape fell out, hitting the floor with a slap. Nancy bent to pick it up. As she straightened, she looked back and saw that the shadow outside had moved. Standing in the doorway was Mayor Abbott's skinny "caretaker," one hand on the door and the other wrapped around his shotgun.

Before the man could get to her, Nancy climbed back inside the dumbwaiter, sending it up to the tower office. She knew Abbott had someone waiting for her there, too, but she hoped the upstairs guy didn't have a gun.

Now she wasn't in a hurry at all, and the dumbwaiter's ascent seemed horribly fast. Just before she reached the top, Nancy stuck the tape in a corner. Whoever was up there had probably guessed about the tape. But if he didn't see it on her, maybe she could pretend not to know anything about it. It's worth a try, she told herself, taking a deep breath as the dumbwaiter came to a stop.

"Well, Miss Drew," Mayor Abbott said as she climbed out. "We meet again."

Nancy kept quiet, wondering how much he'd guessed.

"I see you've been very busy since our interview," the mayor commented, pointing to the tape recorder. "Tell me, does your job always involve stripping down walls?"

"If that's what it takes," Nancy told him.

The mayor nodded. "Clever. John Harrington was clever, too. But I guess you already know that."

Nancy didn't answer.

"Come on, Miss Drew, I know you must have discovered a tape on this machine."

A tape that exposes you as a murderer, Nancy thought.

"I didn't plan to kill Harrington," Mayor Abbott told her as if he'd read her mind. "I didn't even plan to hit him. But when he told me that I was finished, that I'd never get a chance to run for office myself, I lost control. I hit him, and when he fell, his head hit an iron doorstop. It was an accident, but I couldn't let anyone know about it. So I dumped the body out the window."

"What about Charles Ogden?" Nancy asked. "How did you get him to go along with your story?"

"Money," the mayor said. "Ogden wanted money. I had plenty to give him, so he agreed to tell the police exactly what I told him. Of course, I knew I couldn't trust him," he said, shaking his head. "He would always have known the truth. So I had to get rid of him. I'm afraid that right after he left town, Ogden met with a fatal accident."

Nancy closed her eyes. She felt sorry and glad for Hannah at the same time. It was going to be awful for Hannah to know that the man she'd thought of marrying had actually taken money to cover up Harrington's murder. But maybe learning that Ogden wasn't much of a person would help her get over the fact that he'd been murdered.

"Miss Drew." Mayor Abbott broke into her thoughts. "I want that tape."

"I don't have any tape," Nancy lied. "I didn't know about any of this until just now, when you told me." Forget the tape, she was thinking. If he just doesn't find it, then you can tell the police where it is after you get out of here. *If* you get out of here.

"Somehow, I find that hard to believe," the mayor said. "But it doesn't really matter. Tape or no tape, I'm afraid that what happened to Ogden is going to happen to you, too."

Behind him, in the open doorway, the man with the shotgun appeared.

"There's someone downstairs, you know,"

Nancy said. "And a gun like that makes a really loud noise. How are you going to explain it?"

"I'm surprised at you, Miss Drew," the mayor said. "Did you really think you'd have that 'accident' here? You must think I'm stupid. No, you'll be found some distance from the mansion, and by that time, I'll be safely back in my office. No one saw me come in here, and no one's going to see me leave."

No one saw *me*, either, Nancy thought. The best she could do was scream and hope that Barry heard her over the thunder.

"Please, Miss Drew," the mayor said, holding out his hand as if he were her dance partner. "I have a very important meeting in an hour. Let's not waste any more time."

Taking a deep breath, Nancy opened her mouth and gave the most piercing scream she could manage. A clap of thunder drowned it out, but in the split-second that the startled mayor and his henchman paused, Nancy pushed the button and jumped into the dumbwaiter.

She heard a shout followed by a slap. Someone had just hit the panel in frustration.

Good, Nancy thought. Let's just hope this crate makes it to the bottom before they do. If it didn't, she'd be a sitting duck the second the dumbwaiter stopped.

For a few moments Nancy tried to decide if she could get past the two men. The mayor looked out of shape—one good, unexpected push would probably send him sprawling. But his sidekick? The man was skinny, but he looked strong. Besides, he had a gun.

Still, Nancy knew she'd have to fight. Go after the sidekick first, she told herself. If you can get him, the mayor'll be a piece of cake.

Moving as deeply into the dumbwaiter as possible, Nancy braced her foot against the back wall. She was planning to push out the minute the door opened. If she came out fighting, she might catch them off guard.

Suddenly the dumbwaiter stopped. It was so abrupt that Nancy fell over, landing awkwardly on her side. Quickly she tried to get back into position before she opened the door, but then she realized that it didn't matter. The dumbwaiter had stopped, but not in the kitchen.

The power must have gone off. Either the storm had knocked it out or one of those guys had done it. But however it had happened, the dumbwaiter was suspended somewhere between the floors of Harrington House. And Nancy was trapped inside.

Chapter

Sixteen

Nancy fought to keep from panicking. It was one thing to be in that cramped box while it was moving, but to be stuck in it, not knowing how or when she'd get out, was a completely different story.

Nancy took a couple of slow, deep breaths and told herself to calm down. The power couldn't stay off forever. If the storm had done it, it might take hours, but it would still come back on. In the meantime, she knew she wouldn't suffocate.

What if the mayor had remembered where the circuit breaker was and shut the power off? But what reason could he possibly have to do it? To get her so scared she'd fall apart and actually be glad to see him when he let her out?

Fat chance, she thought, sitting up straighter. What other reason could he have? If it weren't for the storm raging outside, all Nancy would have to do would be to scream and kick hard enough, and eventually somebody would hear her. In fact, she wondered, what was she waiting for? It wasn't thundering every second. If she made enough noise, maybe Barry would hear her.

With a piercing shriek, Nancy kicked her heels against the floor of the dumbwaiter and banged the walls with her fists, making so much noise her ears started ringing. Then she stopped and listened.

Nothing but thunder and wind. She started yelling again, and again.

The third time, the heel of her running shoe stuck. Looking down, she saw that she'd kicked so hard, she'd splintered the floor.

Pulling hard, Nancy pried her foot loose. A small section of the floor came up with it. She expected to see nothing but air where the wood had been. Instead, she saw what looked like a white box.

Quickly Nancy reached down and pried loose another piece of wood. She was right—it *was* a box. Four boxes, in fact, each one the perfect size for a reel of tape.

Lifting the boxes out, Nancy had to smile. John Harrington had found the perfect hiding place for his blackmail tapes—a false bottom in the floor of the dumbwaiter, where no one would ever discover them. No one, that is, except a person who happened to get trapped in there during an electrical storm.

But was she still trapped? After all, if she'd been able to break the false bottom so easily, maybe she could break through the real bottom. It would be a long haul down the cable, but anything was better than sitting and waiting for something to happen.

On her hands and knees, Nancy began prying up more of the false bottom until she had an opening she thought she could squeeze through. Then, she kicked at the floor beneath. It gave a little. She kicked harder, wishing she could stand up and give it all her strength.

Finally the wood gave. By kicking again and again, Nancy eventually gouged out a second hole. It was rough and ragged around the edges, but she didn't care how many splinters she got or how much skin she left behind. Nothing mattered but getting out of there.

Nancy reached for the tape she'd found on the recorder and tucked it securely into her waistband. She'd have to leave the other tapes behind, but not this one. This one was leaving Harrington House with her.

On her knees again, Nancy reached through the hole until she could feel the cable. It's probably seventy-five years old at least, she thought. I hope it doesn't pick tonight to break.

Turning around, Nancy began to lower herself feet first into the darkness of the dumbwaiter shaft. She wrapped her legs around the cable, then lowered the rest of her body inch by inch.

Finally Nancy let go of the floor and put all her weight on the cable. Her hands were slick, and she slid a few inches before she managed to stop. Above her the dumbwaiter swayed slightly, and she had to force herself not to climb back into it. It was an awful place to be stuck in, but at least it was more solid than the empty darkness below her. Just keep going, she ordered herself and began to inch her way down the cable.

After a few minutes the muscles in Nancy's arms were shaking badly and her hands felt raw. What she really wanted to do was let go of the cable and drop the rest of the way—anything to stop the ache in her arms. But she had no idea how far she'd come and how much farther she had to go. It can't be too much longer, she kept telling herself. But she knew that if she dropped too soon, the drop might as well be as far as that from a skyscraper.

Nancy tightened her legs around the cable and tried to relax her arms for a second. Then, gritting her teeth, she lowered herself a few more feet.

Suddenly the dumbwaiter swayed hard, bumping against the shaft. Beneath it, Nancy clung to the cable—and felt a nail scrape across her back. The cable slipped from her feet, and for a moment she was hanging by her hands. What's going on? she wondered. Isn't a storm bad enough? Do we have to have an earthquake, too?

Then, above her, Nancy heard Mayor Abbott's voice.

"Miss Drew?" the mayor called. "Can you hear me?"

"Yes," Nancy gasped. "I hear you."

"You sound frightened, Miss Drew."

Terrified is more like it, Nancy thought.

"And I don't blame you for feeling that way," he went on as if she'd answered. "So I propose that we make a deal."

"A deal? What kind of deal?"

"Very simple. You forget what you've discovered about me, and I'll see to it that your bank account suddenly starts growing."

"That's the kind of deal you made with Charles Ogden," Nancy said. "And look what happened to him."

"True, but that's a chance you'll have to take," the mayor said. "And I strongly urge you to take it."

"And if I don't?" Nancy asked.

The mayor chuckled. "Since you can't see us, Miss Drew, I'll describe the situation to you. My assistant is standing right beside me here, and he's holding a hacksaw. Now, the cable to the dumbwaiter may be tough, but it's old, and I'm sure a few good cuts will slice it right in two. I don't really have to tell you what will happen then, do I?"

No, Nancy thought, you don't. Once that cable goes, I'm gone. Wiping her forehead on her sleeve, Nancy took a deep breath. "No deal!" she shouted.

"All right, Miss Drew," the mayor called back. "Have it your way."

There was silence, and then the dumbwaiter and cable began swaying again. Without thinking, Nancy held on tight.

Wait a minute, she told herself. What are you doing? The guy's hacking at this cable and you're holding it as if it were a lifeline!

Well, she'd been wondering exactly how far

down she'd shinnied. Now was her chance to find out. If the drop was too far, it wouldn't matter, anyway. But if she were fairly close to the kitchen, she just might make it.

The dumbwaiter swayed and thumped again, and Nancy knew it wouldn't be long before that hacksaw did its job. If she wanted a chance, she was going to have to take it. *Now.*

Without counting to three, without crossing her fingers, without holding her breath, Nancy loosened her hold on the cable and dropped into the darkness below.

Chapter

Seventeen

WHENEVER NANCY DREAMED she was falling, the fall always seemed endless. But this time she wasn't dreaming, and it took only two seconds before her feet hit the floor so hard it made her teeth hurt. If that's all that hurts, she thought, as she crumpled to her knees, I'm lucky.

Above her, she heard the dumbwaiter creak. Just seconds before it crashed to the bottom, Nancy had rolled out of the shaft and onto the black and white tiles of the kitchen floor.

Before she had a chance to catch her breath, she heard someone cross the room. Then she felt a hand on her arm. Gasping, she struggled to break away. But when she realized whose hand was holding her, she stopped.

"Ned!" she cried, sagging against him. "I was never so glad to see anyone in my life!"

Ned's arms were around her, helping her to stand. Nancy wanted to collapse with relief—but she couldn't. Not yet.

Nancy stumbled to the kitchen phone and picked up the receiver. The line was dead, knocked out by the storm. The only way to let the police in on what was happening was to tell them in person.

"Come on," Nancy said, taking Ned's hand. "We've got to get out of here! Where'd you park your car?"

"Right near yours," Ned said.

"Okay, let's run for it!"

Together, Nancy and Ned burst out of Harrington House and started heading for the stone wall. They hadn't gone more than a few yards when a loud crack filled the air. The storm was still going strong, but Nancy knew it wasn't thunder she had just heard. It was a shotgun.

Glancing over her shoulder, Nancy saw the mayor's sidekick taking aim again. Before he could shoot, the mayor ran up and pushed him away. Then the two of them took off together.

They're going for their car, Nancy thought. And if they get us on that cliff road this time, we'll never make it down.

"Who was that?" Ned asked, running beside her.

"If I have anything to say about it," Nancy told him, gasping for breath, "that'll be the *former* mayor of River Heights."

Ned raised his eyebrows and whistled, but he kept on running.

The wind plastered Nancy's wet hair to her face, and she had to keep peeling it away to see where she was going. She hoped the dogs didn't decide to show up. The only thing she had to give them was the tape, and she wasn't about to let go of that.

Finally they reached the wall and climbed over and into the woods, heading for the road and the cars. "We'll take your car!" Nancy shouted. "I have a feeling mine may be missing another distributor cap!"

Ned jumped into his car and had the engine going before Nancy even opened her door. By the time she got in and closed it, the car was moving, its tires squealing as Ned did a three-point turn on the narrow road.

Ned had just straightened the car out and was about to pull away when he jammed on the brakes so hard that Nancy's seat belt locked against her.

Looking out through the rain-washed windshield, Nancy saw a long gray limousine. She didn't recognize the driver, who had jumped out and was gesturing wildly for them to move. But she did recognize the passenger who stuck his head out the window. It was Todd Harrington.

"What's the problem?" Todd asked, walking over to Ned's car.

"The police!" Nancy told him. "We have to get to the police. You've got to move your car!"

"I have a better idea," Todd said, gesturing for them to come with him.

As Nancy and Ned slid into the limousine next to two members of his campaign staff, Todd pushed a button on the back of the seat. A panel slid down. Inside was a telephone. "Why don't you call them?" Todd suggested with a smile.

Laughing in relief, Nancy punched the number. When Mayor Abbott's car pulled up behind Ned's, a police car was already on the way, its siren screaming as it raced up the cliff road.

"Well, congratulations, Nancy," Brenda Carlton said over the phone a couple of days later. "You won."

"You mean I haven't lost my touch?" Nancy asked jokingly.

"Well, I don't know about that. You have to admit you were awfully lucky."

"So were you," Nancy said, deciding not to argue. "After all, you found Neil Gray."

"That wasn't luck!"

"You mean it was detective work?"

"Oh, all right," Brenda grumbled. "My father knew somebody who knew somebody who knew Neil Gray. That's how I found him." She sighed. "Anyway, now he's safely in jail. I heard his lawyer is going to try for a plea of temporary insanity, but I don't really know. Well, anyway, since I got you into this little detective contest, I thought I ought to congratulate you for winning it."

You mean your father told you to, Nancy thought.

"But don't get too conceited about it," Brenda warned. "I learned a lot on this case. Next time, you'll have a real battle on your hands."

Next time? Nancy wondered after Brenda had hung up. Another detective duel with Brenda Carlton? Never.

Even though Nancy knew she'd have another case, she was sure there'd never be another one like this. Spread out in front of her on the kitchen table were newspapers from the past two days, each one filled with stories about the Harrington case.

Mayor Abbott and his assistant were both in jail, awaiting their trials. Todd was up to his ears in interviews about his father and Mayor Abbott, but he was being charmingly honest about the whole thing, and Nancy figured most people wouldn't blame him for what his father had been.

The hardest part had been telling Hannah about Charles Ogden. Nancy had dreaded it, but when she finally told her, Hannah was very calm. "I'm lucky, in a way," she'd said. "If things had worked out and I'd married Charlie, I probably would have had a miserable life. I would never have met my husband—or come to work for your family." She smiled at Nancy. "And look at the wonderful life I've had."

Nancy smiled, too, remembering what Hannah had said. Then, glancing at her watch, she frowned. She had to go. Ned wanted her to meet him in the park by the river. It was time they had that talk, he'd said.

Before going, Nancy stopped in front of the hall mirror. Her outfit—a long flowered skirt and a green scoop-neck cotton sweater—was one of her favorites. Her hair smelled lemony and her fingernails were freshly polished. She smiled and nodded at her reflection. "If you're going to get dumped," she told herself, "at least you can look good."

Ned was waiting for her when she got to the park. When he saw her, he got up from the bench and walked toward her, smiling and brushing his brown hair back. "Hi," he said, taking her hand. "You look terrific."

"Thanks." Nancy smiled nervously and then decided to get it over with. "Well? What's this serious talk about?"

"Us." Still holding her hand, Ned led her to a bench, and they sat down.

"I figured that," Nancy said. "The other night, right before Hannah came running out of the house, you started to say something. You said, 'This is really hard . . .' Why don't you finish the sentence now?"

"I remember," Ned said. "I've been thinking about us all the time I've been home. At first, I just wasn't sure whether we ought to stay together. But the more I saw you, the more I realized I wanted to be with you. And it was hard, because you were so busy with the case and everything. I even worried about asking you out—I didn't want it to seem as though I was trying to take you away from your job."

"It's probably always going to be that way, Ned," Nancy told him.

"I know, and that's okay," Ned said. "It was just hard, because all I wanted to do was put my arms around you. That's still all I want to do."

Sighing in relief, Nancy grinned at him. "So who's stopping you now?" she asked.

Grinning back, Ned wrapped his arms around her and held her tightly.

"By the way," Nancy whispered, "I never did ask you why you came to Harrington House that day."

Ned laughed softly. "I came to tell you that I love you," he said.

Just before they kissed, Nancy thought that maybe she hadn't lost *this* touch, either.

Nancy's next case:

An investigation at a Texas oilman's ranch sounds as if it's something out of a TV show. But as Nancy probes the mystery of the millionaire's long-lost daughter, she finds a family with more secrets than a prime-time soap!

What is the millionaire's new wife hiding? What are his stepson's plans for taking over the ranch? Why is the longtime housekeeper acting so suspiciously?

As Nancy tries to find answers, she becomes the target of a series of accidents. That's bad enough. But then she becomes the target of bullets . . . in *HEART OF DANGER*, Case #11 in The Nancy Drew Files™.